Also by Patti Angeletti

Preflight: A Soul Prepares to Return to Earth
Rising Above Organized Religion: The Journey to the Higher View
(as Patti Murphy)

LANDING

A Soul Embarks on a Life on Earth

Patti Angeletti

iUniverse, Inc.

Bloomington

Copyright © 2010 Patti Angeletti

All rights reserved. No part of this book may be used or reproduced by any means, graphic, electronic, or mechanical, including photocopying, recording, taping or by any information storage retrieval system without the written permission of the publisher except in the case of brief quotations embodied in critical articles and reviews.

This is a work of fiction. All of the characters, names, incidents, organizations, and dialogue in this novel are either the products of the author's imagination or are used fictitiously.

iUniverse books may be ordered through booksellers or by contacting:

iUniverse
1663 Liberty Drive
Bloomington, IN 47403
www.iuniverse.com
1-800-Authors (1-800-288-4677)

Because of the dynamic nature of the Internet, any Web addresses or links contained in this book may have changed since publication and may no longer be valid. The views expressed in this work are solely those of the author and do not necessarily reflect the views of the publisher, and the publisher hereby disclaims any responsibility for them.

ISBN: 978-1-4502-6650-5 (pbk)
ISBN: 978-1-4502-6648-2 (cloth)
ISBN: 978-1-4502-6649-9 (ebk)

Printed in the United States of America

iUniverse rev. date: 11/16/2010

In memory of those we have been and continue to be. For all who believe in unseen influences, spirits, angels, déjà vu, everlasting life, and, most of all, love.

"Because in the school of the Spirit, man learns
wisdom through humility, knowledge by forgetting,
how to speak by silence, how to live by dying."

—Johannes Tauler

PREFACE

Are you thinking that this New Age/metaphysical stuff is just not for you? Have you thought that it is just a scheme to take your money or make fools of men? Yes, I will admit that there are many in the world that are not the "real deal" and will do anything for a buck. Why do you think that is? Well, it is because they can. Do they get away with it? Yes, they do.

That is why discernment is so important. Believing in your own inner guidance and "gut" when an idea or situation arises can be very beneficial. In fact, at times it is lifesaving. It is important to trust yourself and let go of the beliefs of those who may not have your best interest at heart. It comes with listening, feeling, and learning for yourself your own truths.

If you choose to read and enjoy even a small portion of this book and the music you hear, listen with your heart. Open your mind to the ideas and possibilities. Not all lessons are for your benefit and not all ideas are meant for you (or maybe just not at this time). However, there may be some truth here for you.

If you feel anything that remotely sounds familiar—that you have thought about before and dismissed as false—try it on for size again. See if it fits just a little better. Give it a test drive.

Maybe now it will feel right. What would be the harm in finding something wonderful, some truth for yourself that expands your mind and soul, brings you more peace and love and forgiveness for yourself and others? Nothing whatsoever. You and the world would be better for it.

How do you face the fears and challenges in life? Do you think it would have made a difference if you had known from birth what was ahead of you? Perhaps not knowing is wise because otherwise you might be too discouraged and disheartened at what was in store for you.

Our souls face many challenges. I do not believe that they come to us by chance. I believe that situations occur in our lives by divine intervention in order that we may grow spiritually, mentally, and emotionally. I believe that if we face our lessons with a strong heart and desire to make good of it, we will grow in every way. When that occurs, we experience more love for ourselves and share greater love and understanding with others.

One of the best things about our existence is the ability and opportunity to choose. We use free will in making choices that may result in wondrous things or absolute disasters. I believe that we are ultimately responsible for what we choose and how we feel about all things. In a lighthearted exchange between the characters in my previous book *Preflight*, the souls sing, "You get to choose where you will go when you're in the human race," and "Life is just a game, we play with no winners or losers." They encourage each other to "play nice." I share that advice with the world.

I have a very strong sense of connectedness with the universe and everything in it. I believe my thoughts and actions create a ripple effect that travels out from me and touches everything in some way. That alone causes me to think more seriously about what I say and do, how I allow myself to feel about things, and even where I go. Again, this causes me to be a more thinking and doing being, rather than one that simply reacts. In this way, I feel that I am ultimately more conscious.

This book comes from my thoughts about our connectedness as souls and the possibility of soul families that interact over and over again through reincarnation. My desire is to share with you, dear reader, the story of a girl born to her selected parents, particular souls who agreed before their earthly time to connect physically and spiritually in order to assist their souls to grow.

My desire is that you enjoy the story and the music, if nothing else. Hasn't there been a time when you heard a song and remembered where you were the first time you heard it? Do you recall a drive in a car with the radio blasting with your own mix of road music? Do you remember being in a restaurant and hearing a song that took your mind to another place and time, to a concert or a dance? Music helps tell the story of our own lives. The lyrics and music in this book do that as well.

In order to begin any serious journey, it is important that preparations take place. Fortunately for this story, many of the same characters in *Preflight: A Soul Prepares to Return to Earth* have completed some of the preliminary work (while in spirit) of coordinating their moves, their choices, and much of their interaction with each other. They made preparations and intentions known to share and grow through certain events and aspects of their lives.

It is time to step back just a few years so that the proper stage can be set for Sarah, the incoming spirit and central figure of *Preflight: A Soul Prepares to Return to Earth*. Enjoy the ongoing story of Beth and Joe and how they met in order that Sarah might realize the plans that she and other soul family members made while spirits in another reality.

CONTENTS

To Divine Intervention, inspiration and guidance of my personal angels and guides. It brings me great peace knowing they have always been there for me, to assist me with pure love in helping me find joy in this story.

To my music director, Frank Casian, who took this project on with his heart and soul. He caught the vision of my lyrics and brought his incredible talent in a melding of magic.

To vocalists Cindy B. Lemas, Jamie Peters, and Hugh Connolly, who brought life to the characters. You have amazed and touched my soul.

To talented musicians Frank, Hugh, Sean Van Buskirk, and David Sinclair, who added their own inspiration to every song.

To Calvin Turnbull at Old School Studio in Caspar, California, who shared gift in the creation of the music CD.

To my own lessons of life, which have forged me in the fire and brought me to the incredible place I am today.

INTRODUCTION

The Lullaby,
the sweet melodious sounds made by all of creation,
reminding us that we are one.

Areanna

I will be the storyteller for much of this book—me and the other guardian angels of the primary souls in this story. My name is Areanna. I am an angel. More specifically, I am Sarah's guardian angel, and I will add a perspective and experiences to the story that you may not have imagined. Please allow me (and other angels) to give you another view, another dimension to earth life and beyond. It may assist you in remembering or imagining your own life and experiences in a different way.

There is much that goes on behind the scenes or beyond the memory of the souls on earth. My associates, guardian angels, personal guides, and others will be assisting the souls. Many of the souls decided in the spirit world—prior to their individual incarnations—to interact with each other in order to help them learn the lessons they chose to experience. This interaction gives their souls an opportunity to expand and grow.

What would it be like to completely forget who you are, what you are here to do, or why you arrived at a particular place at a particular time? How would it feel to exist in a type of mental fog without knowing that you are in one? Would you find it strange to have moments of clarity or glimpses of truth that caused you to think that you were seeing things or feeling things that could not possibly be true? This type of forgetting begins when you leave the spirit world and arrive as a newborn on Earth. This amnesia begins at birth.

Babies arrive with what could be described as an essence of innocence. They are not able to express themselves for quite some time—except by crying, which works well in order to get attention and motivate someone to do something about anything that may be troubling them. There have been many parents and grandparents who have wished that their little ones could just speak and tell them exactly what is causing their distress. This would make raising them much simpler. Many others have wished for more—that these beautiful tiny ones could tell the world about the place that they recently left, the souls and beings that surround them, and what perfect love is about.

Do these little ones remember from their arrival at birth that they decided to take a leap of faith and present themselves on Earth for another round of experiences and lessons? No, they did not forget, but their memory of "home" dims over time and, because of their limited way of communicating, they are not able to tell you the wondrous things that they already know. If newborns could express themselves in more than just cries or coos, they could share a great deal of information that would surprise those of you who have forgotten everything. As a baby grows and its language improves, many have been known to share a story or two about previous incarnations, about specific family members now and in other lives (where they lived, what they did, etc.), and what supposedly unseen things they see and feelings that they are experiencing. How could these stories be contrived when they seem to have no point of reference?

Allow me to explain the Lullaby. It is a beautiful, etheric melody that assists souls in remembering. It reminds them of a place of utter joy and love—a place where all beings are connected. The Lullaby has been described as a pure resonance, sounding similar to a symphony of crystal violins that all creatures in the universe recognize. It is a part of everyone and everything, experienced through the mind, heart, and soul with the deepest sensations of love and joy. It has the power to heal all wounds, emotional and physical.

Chapter 1:
Destiny in a Tree

"Help! Somebody help, please."

This fearful cry, followed by a faint whimper, traveled through the air, almost like a whisper. Beth thought that she heard it, but wasn't sure whether someone was just messing around. The wind was blowing through the trees on that hot summer afternoon, birds were singing, and faint traffic noise was brought to her consciousness as she enjoyed a candy bar while relaxing in a green and brown lawn chair. There was a television on next door, but she didn't think the cry was coming from it.

Beth had been sitting for quite a while, so bored with the afternoon that the straps of the lawn chair had made deep marks on the back of her thighs. And she really didn't care right then. Her mother, Jill, didn't let her have candy very often, so Beth thought that she had better eat slowly and really enjoy her treat.

Someone needing help could potentially be a big deal. Sweet River was a sleepy little farming community and the only home Beth had ever known. Nothing too exciting happened there, unless you count the time triplets were born at the hospital where her mother worked or the time a famous actor's car broke down and he ate at Strikes & Burgers, the local hangout that combined two American icons: bowling and hamburgers, while waiting for his car to be repaired.

"Help!"

This time Beth knew that it was real and could tell the general direction that it was coming from. She ran to the street from the backyard from under one of the massive weeping willows trees that lined her lot. The shade was a great place to escape from the midsummer heat, a place to daydream and enjoy her Twix.

"Where are you?" Beth yelled to her left. A faint and somehow familiar voice whimpered, "Up here. In the tree!"

Beth knew that the house down the block with the large maple tree in front had been vacant for some time. As she ran gingerly over the hot pavement with bare feet, her steps were quick enough to keep her feet from blistering. Surprisingly enough, Beth hardly felt more than warmth. Her feet had developed thick soles from walking without shoes through the warmer months of the year. She could not get away from wearing shoes outside in the winter (her parents would not allow that) and, of course, she had to wear them to school. But as soon as Beth walked through the door, her shoes were off. You could always find at least one pair by the Greens' front door.

As she got closer, she noticed that the "For Rent" sign was lying on the sidewalk and a U-Haul truck was parked in the driveway. Next to it was parked an old green Ford pickup. There were boxes everywhere on the lawn and driveway, but no one could be seen.

Beth looked up from the base of one of the maple trees. She saw two legs dangling, feet frantically kicking the air like a swimmer paddling in water.

"I'm coming," she bravely called out.

"I can't get down. I'm stuck," the boy whimpered. He sounded frightened and vulnerable when he heard Beth's approach.

Beth was an experienced tree climber despite only being nine. Her average frame was lean and strong, her hands and arms were covered with scratches, and her lower legs showed bruises in various colors and sizes. Being active was part of her nature. Her parents had given up trying to keep her from exploring the world of caves, rivers, and cliffs.

As she quickly sized up the tree, Beth found the best branches to make her ascent and readily make her way to the stranded climber. She encouraged him with words of support as she worked her way upward through the maze. "You're going to be fine. Don't worry. I'm coming. I will help you."

As Beth got closer, she noticed that his legs were thin and pale. *He must not get out in the sun much,* Beth thought. As she climbed up further in the tree, she was now able to look at the stranded boy's face. Beth saw dusty, tear-stained cheeks and the biggest brown eyes she had ever seen. There was something immediately familiar about them, but she didn't want to think about that as they looked pleadingly at her. She wanted to focus on how she needed to help him.

The boy saw a sense of confidence in the demeanor of the girl with extremely curly, long dark blonde hair. He couldn't help but notice it as it fell over her face and down her shoulders. It reminded him of very long sheep hair. When he saw her light green eyes, he thought that he might have met her before somewhere. He dismissed that thought quickly, knowing that he would have easily remembered anyone with hair like that. Besides, he was new in town and could sure use a friend right now. He was impressed with her climbing skills, but felt his face suddenly flush, embarrassed to ask for help from a girl.

"I can't get down. My shorts are stuck on a branch," the boy practically whispered to her.

Beth quickly sized up the situation. It seemed to her that this novice climber was on his way down from climbing the tree when the back of his shorts got caught on a small, short branch. As he had attempted to lower himself, the fabric stretched and his feet lost their perch, which had caused his predicament.

"I can't let go or I'll fall." He held desperately to the tree, both arms wrapped around a branch—unable to reach back and free himself—thus giving himself a perfectly executed wedgie.

A slow smile spread across Beth's face when she realized what she was seeing. She had given and received many wedgies, but had never seen a tree do it. It took a bit of restraint on her part to keep from laughing out loud.

"I'll have to cut your shorts. It's the only way." Beth produced a small pocketknife from her back pocket. Her father had given it to her on her eighth birthday, thinking that it was a perfect gift for a budding tomboy. Beth's mother, Jill, disagreed, countering that gift with a doll, hoping that her little girl would prefer the more feminine toy. Needless to say, the doll remained propped on a shelf in Beth's bedroom, and the pocketknife accompanied its owner on many adventures. This one would now top the list of the funny ways that she had used the useful tool.

"No! You'll cut me!" The boy produced another whimper. Beth only smiled again.

"Oh, I will not," said Beth with annoyance. "Do you want to get down? I could just go home and not tell anyone where you are."

"No!" the boy cried, and a new stream of tears coursed down his cheeks. He hated that he was crying, especially in front of a girl. Beth knew that it would be rude to make fun of him. Since her mother never used anyone's misfortune as an opportunity to laugh and taught her daughter to do the same, Beth simply gave him a kind look. That seemed to ease his fears. "Okay, just be careful."

"Hold the branch tight with your arms and don't move. This should only take a second." Beth bit her tongue in concentration as she skillfully slit through the back of his pants. Just as the damaged fabric could no longer support his weight, the boy started to lose his grip on the branch. When he started his sudden descent, Beth's knife struck flesh.

"Ow!"

"Sorry, I'm so sorry. I've almost got it. Don't let go of the branch!" Beth continued to bite her tongue, with her eyes focused only on the task at hand. "Just a little more."

The tearing of fabric was heard as the entire back of his shorts tore away, revealing Spider-Man underwear. Beth's eyes opened wide, and then she chuckled quietly. The boy was able to find a branch to stand on, and he quickly sat down in order to hide the back of his shorts. He opened his mouth to thank her, but stopped as he heard a voice yelling.

"Joe! What are you doing up in that tree?" A husky male voice called from the ground, sounding somewhat angry, yet amused. He saw his son sitting on the branch with a girl standing near him. "There must be a little of me in you after all!"

"Dad! I got stuck. I'm sorry. She came to help me out," Joe rapidly explained.

Joe quickly made it to the ground, despite having only a semblance of shorts on his thin frame. A small trail of blood started seeping from the wound on his right buttock, and a large red spot appeared on Spider-Man. He tried to hide the back of his pants and his wound, but his father quickly spun him around.

"What's this?" Joe's father said while taking a brief look at the cut. "Looks like this will need stitches. Grab a rag in the house and get in the truck." Joe quickly ran to the house, limping just a little as pain from the wound caught up with him.

Beth stood in silence after she jumped to the ground from the lowest branch. A giant of a man towered over her. He was the tallest and biggest man she had ever seen. His dark hair resembled his sons, but his frame reminded her of Andre the Giant. She was thinking that she should run home quickly, but his smile was sincere and his eyes were kind. She realized that she had nothing to fear as he said kindly, "Thank you, young lady, for helping my boy. What is your name?"

With a whisper and a slight croak she replied, "Beth."

"Is that short for Elizabeth?"

"Yes."

"We just moved in. I guess you can see that. Anyway, thanks again."

"Sure. Okay. Hey, sorry about the cut. Don't worry. Stitches don't hurt too much," Beth called out to Joe as he climbed slowly into the truck and sat on the uninjured buttock.

"Let me know how many stitches you get. I bet I've got ya beat," Beth challenged.

Not smiling and staring straight ahead, Joe simply nodded his head. His cheeks glowed a brilliant red, which the hot summer breeze did not cool down. His father joined him in the vehicle. With a noisy start, the old truck made its way down the street.

***

Later that afternoon, Beth heard the rumble of the truck as it pulled into the driveway three houses away. She trotted down the sidewalk and greeted Joe as he exited the passenger side.

"How did it go?" Beth asked, bending her head slightly to get into Joe's face with her questioning look.

Joe avoided her gaze and his face reddened as his father answered.

"Four stitches. Yeah, little lady, you sure know how to use a knife," Joe's father chuckled. "No hard feelings, really."

"Okay. That's good. Only four? I told you that I would beat you. I've had twelve, but not on my butt," Beth explained.

The man said, "Hell of a way to make friends in the neighborhood. Oops, sorry for the language. We Neal men haven't been around any ladies for a while, and I forget to watch what I say."

7

"That's okay. I don't mind. I'm not much of a *lady* anyway. My parents don't think so," Beth said.

The man went on. "So the vet clinic was pretty accommodating. I knew it would cost more if we went to the emergency room. It's great to live in a small town. Lots of perks."

"You had the vet sew him up?" Beth's eyes opened wide as her jaw dropped. She saw a faint smile on the big man's face. She glanced over at Joe and saw him roll his big brown eyes skyward and slowly shake his head, obviously annoyed.

"I don't think I introduced myself before. My name's Steve. Steve Neal. I'm just pulling your leg about the vet." Beth shook his rough, beefy right hand, which was extended in a friendly gesture.

"Well, that's okay. I told my mom about you guys and she wants to meet you. I'll go get her," Beth said.

"Hurry, cause I've got to finish movin' the rest of this stuff in the house and get the truck back to the rental place before five," Steve replied.

Beth quickly ran down the street and began to yell as she got closer to her house.

"Mom, they're back!" Beth could be heard down the entire street. Joe was glad that there weren't any other neighbors outside.

Beth soon returned, walking beside a tall, thin woman with a pie in one hand and a big smile on her face. She was wearing hospital scrubs with bumblebees on them. Even though she had only a little makeup on, she was still attractive, and her eyes were bright and friendly. She had the same curly hair as her daughter, but cut very short.

"I'm Jill Green. I have to meet all the new neighbors. Want you to feel welcome," Jill explained. "If Beth will be playing with your son, I like to get to know the parents. Sorry, but that's just how I am. A little cautious, I guess. Hope you don't mind." Her straightforward style suited Steve just fine.

Steve smiled and replied quickly, "Nice to meet you. Oh, no. I don't mind a bit. Can't blame you there. Crazy world we live in. Can't be too careful. I'm Steve Neal. My boy here is Joe."

"Nice to meet you." A strong handshake followed and the pie was offered. "It's still frozen. Sorry. No time to thaw it out. I keep several in the freezer—just for times like this," Jill explained.

"Well, thanks. That's very nice of you. Did you bake it yourself?" Steve seemed impressed.

"No. I'm not that much of a Betty Crocker. I get them in bulk when I travel to the city about once a month. They are cheaper that way," explained Jill. "Where are you folks from?"

"We just came from Northern California—been several places there. My family goes way back with the logging industry. I'm a logger. Jobs have been drying up, so we thought we'd come here and give the mill a try."

"Oh, that's great! My husband, Bill, works at Hawk Mill and Storage," Jill said with a sense of feigned pride. "I'm sure you'll meet him. He's one of the swing shift supervisors."

Steve looked at Jill's scrubs. "You must be a nurse?"

"Yes, for quite a few years now. I work at the hospital. We take care of pretty much everything around here. Sometimes we ship people out to the bigger hospitals in the area. It isn't easy taking care of people you know—small town and all. We're like a big family."Joe and Beth, becoming bored by the adult conversation, started to look at each other's feet. Joe noticed Beth's obvious deep tan and lack of shoes.

"Don't you ever wear shoes?" Joe asked.

"Nah. Never really liked shoes—even as a baby. Always pulling them off. Mom lets me go without them most of the time. Want to see how tough the bottoms are?" Beth sat on the grass and lifted her right foot.

"No, that's okay," Joe said. "Maybe later."

"Mom, can I take Joe and show him around for a while?" Beth asked, interrupting the adult conversation.

"That's okay with me, but you'll have to be back before I leave for work. Are you okay with that, Steve? Should we ask your wife?" Jill asked.

Steve said, "That's fine. You kids take off. Just don't sit down and bust open those stitches, Joe."

"Okay, Dad."

When the children were out of earshot, Steve said, "There isn't a wife. I don't like to talk about it much, but you might as well know. Joe's mother left him with me when he was little. Joe doesn't even remember her. She didn't like the woods—said it was too rustic for her. She wanted more glamour and took off for San Francisco. A few years ago, I heard she got some disease and died. The only mother Joe ever knew is his great aunt, Misty. She was my father's sister. She still lives out in Northern California."

"I'm sorry for your troubles. I hope you and Joe like it here. If there's anything you need or want to know about the town, you can ask me. We've been here forever," Jill said with a laugh.

"That's very kind. You've done plenty today. That's quite the daughter you have." Steve looked down the street as the children got to the corner of the block.

"Yes, one of a kind, that Beth," Jill said.

"Well, I'd better get busy. Thanks again for the pie." Steve shook Jill's hand again and turned toward the house.

"You're are welcome. I'll see you around."

You're My Best Friend

Sun's up, it's a brand new day
Time to go on out and play
It's great we're not in school
And not have to worry 'bout the teachers' rules

We could hang out at the park
Stay out till it gets dark
Got a tent up at my place
Bet I could beat you in a race

(Chorus)
We want to find adventure
In the places that we go
It might be a little scary
But the best thing that I know
You're my best friend

(When they are thirteen years old)
Help me study for this test
My grades this year are a mess
I'd rather be hearing some tunes
Or riding our bikes at the dunes

(When they are seventeen years old)
We love to stare up at the stars
What would life be like on Mars?
Learning to drive was fun
I'll be glad when high school's done

(Chorus)

Got a feeling that's true to the end
You're my best friend
Come hang around with me
You're my best friend
It's gonna be great
You'll see

CHAPTER 2:
DESTINY FROM THE
ANGELS' VIEW

Areanna

The tree incident occurred with Beth and Joe's angels watching with great intent and anticipation. Angels are watching constantly—regardless of the place or time. Because this was such a momentous occasion for Beth and Joe, their primary guardian angels were especially present to intervene in order to keep Beth and Joe safe from any further danger. Mesha and Kamali, Beth and Joe's angels respectively, would have prevented the two children from falling from the tree, for example. That was not part of the plan for this event.

Sarah (my charge and future child of Beth and Joe's) and I were very interested in watching as everything unfolded and found it very entertaining. Sarah was not included in much of the pre-life planning Beth and Joe completed while in spirit. It was not necessary, and Sarah trusted that her soul family members would meet on Earth at some time. You may call it destiny, but choices and life paths are not necessarily predestined in all cases. Even one change can affect many lives and situations, but it is all in perfect order regardless.

As a soul is presented with choices, they are allowed to determine their reaction or course of action. Even doing nothing is a choice—a choice to do no-thing. Sometimes the choices individuals make are conscious and at other times they seem completely unconscious. Either way is perfect. Each choice brings a soul further down their path toward other choices. Life on Earth is absolutely full of them.

When Sarah decided that she wanted to return to Earth for another incarnation, she ultimately gathered her soul family members together. They used the Possibilities Board. The process of using the Possibilities Board is quite exciting and very interesting.

The Possibilities Board is like nothing you could create on Earth. It is energy held into position by thought and cooperation. The shape is determined by the number of souls involved in using it, and it contracts and expands as souls move around it. It is not even a flat surface, but can be pushed down or pulled up into various shapes, as needed.

If I could compare it to anything on Earth that you may recognize and relate to, it would be like a flexible Plexiglas surface, approximately two inches thick. Again, the outer dimensions could range anywhere from two feet to thirty feet.

The upper surface could be compared to a game board, with various trails or spaces to move in. Holographic images of towns, roads, continents, etc. are fluid-like and capable of moving, expanding, and contracting. There are even spaces that represent time dimension (hour, month, day, year, etc.).

Each soul has a token that represents itself. The piece resembles the physical body that the soul will occupy on Earth—even to the point of taking on the appearance of aging. Every soul moves its token with a thought. New paths open and others may close as each soul expresses its desires or choices for its life, including how it might interact with other souls. As the glowing piece moves about the board, it can become brighter or dimmer as the possibility for a planned lesson becomes more or less of a reality in a certain time or place in the soul's life. A pink light surrounds the individual tokens whenever a soul interacts with its soul family members. The souls then discuss the main purpose of that particular meeting. Choices and possibilities are discussed as well.

The level of cooperation is like no other. There is no ego to influence decisions. Each move is made with love and everyone is mindful of the ultimate goal. The end goal is for the soul to learn lessons, and this is done by interactions in life in myriad circumstances and events.

As mentioned before, even though the Possibilities Board resembles a game board, there is no competition, no desire for dominance or winning, and no score to keep. There is no right or wrong way either.

We angels are present as support to the soul for all life experiences. We extend perfect and unconditional love—even when it is not felt. We are there to whisper encouragement and guidance at times. We do our part when we have been asked to do so since it is our job to serve. However, our knowing extends beyond earthly remembrance and in that way we give the soul the opportunity to "suffer the consequences" of choices that are for growth when that is what the soul chose for itself prior to being incarnated. In other words, we do not interfere if the soul has a desire to experience something and we were previously asked to stand by.

So, let us return to Joe and Beth. Soon after their meeting in the tree, we three angels met to discuss the incident.

***

"I wasn't so sure that the knife was a good idea." Mesha's lavender gossamer wings made a soft whooshing sound as she approached Kamali. "I told Beth that specifically when we were planning this introduction to Joe. And it really isn't up to me how she and Joe decided to meet, as you know. I only advised Beth on plans and possible outcomes.

"Beth decided she wanted to use the knife anyway. That is why she was so happy to get the knife as a gift from her father," Mesha explained. "Beth remembered that somehow or in some way, the knife was going to come in handy and she would want it in the future."

Kamali, an angel with pale blue, iridescent wings with a fuchsia hue, hovered next to Joe, her charge. Joe, unaware of the conversation, slept soundly. It was a peaceful, moonlit night only a month after Joe and his father had arrived in Sweet River.

"Well, Beth is pretty adventuresome. That is just her nature and she has always had that part of her personality in most lifetimes. Joe already knew that—considering they have been in the same soul family and have had many incarnations together," Kamali replied. A knowing smile spread across Kamali's face as she remembered the planning sessions Beth and Joe had had before coming to Earth this time.

Kamali explained, "Joe thought that getting a little cut on his behind by Beth's knife at their first meeting might be something funny that the two of them could laugh about later. But the moment Beth nicked him, he wasn't laughing, was he?"

"No, he wasn't," I replied with a chuckle. "Sarah thought the whole scene was pretty funny as we watched it unfold. Sarah wasn't told everything—just that her parents were going to meet as children. It is interesting to recall the various lifetimes Beth and Joe have been Sarah's parents."

"Oh, they are very attached within their soul family—that is for sure," Mesha stated. "They are committed to assisting in whatever way they can to help their souls grow—and we are just as committed to be with them and do what we can."

"It is certainly a joy to help them. Mesha, was it a challenge to orchestrate Steve's move to Sweet River?" I asked.

"Free will is always acknowledged and respected," Mesha explained. "The soul would not be able to grow through experiences and challenges without it. Steve, on Earth and having forgotten pre-planning here, was unsure what would be the best for him and Joe. He had considered a different town other than Sweet River at one point. But every time he would think about Sweet River and learned more about it, I would whisper in his ear, 'Yes,' and he would experience a warm, calm sensation throughout his

19

body. He was not always receptive to the promptings. When he finally made his decision, he knew that it was the right one. I simply offered Steve an opportunity to remember how he moved himself around the Possibilities Board. It is not up to us to force any soul to make choices."

Kamali moved across the room and concentrated on a photograph in an open box. Joe, as a baby, was being held in the arms of a beautiful young woman with a sweet smile. Her eyes were the same color as Joe's—a deep brown with flecks of gold. In the photo, the woman had a look of wonder as she gazed into the camera, as if the camera captured a moment in time of confusion, exhaustion, and relief. Joe was literally only hours old.

"These situations on Earth can cause such pain and heartache. I realize that Joe wanted to grow up without a mother and be raised by Steve alone in order to learn about abandonment. Knowing that angels are present to do our jobs and offer solace and peace is truly a blessing. I love what we do," Kamali stated.

"Remember that Steve was in agreement for this lesson as well," I replied.

"Of course. Steve also wanted to learn more about being abandoned and becoming a single parent. He had left his families in other incarnations, so he thought it would be helpful for him to better understand the other side of that lesson." Kamali moved closer to Joe and gently stroked his cheek. Joe took in a deeper breath and smiled, as if dreaming about something wonderful.

Teneaka, Steve's guardian angel, joined us. Teneaka liked to appear as a Roman soldier in full battle gear and his wings appeared to be liquid silver. His eyes shined with a kindness that belied his external appearance, and his aura glowed of pure love.

"It seems that Steve has been doing well raising Joe on his own. He has been patient with Joe, showing him by example what is important in this life: kindness, love, sharing, and listening. There will be more challenges for them, but, so far, they have weathered the challenges that have come," said Teneaka.

"Yes, they have," agreed Kamali. "The basis of their relationship is love. We could not ask for more."

Celestial Flight Crew

(Areanna)
We've been doin' our work
For an eternity
Blessing and guiding
God's family

(Mesha)
Helping the souls
Under our care
Knowing your pain
We're well aware

(Kamali)
The lessons, the karma
The challenges you face
Dealing with life
And your fast pace

(Areanna)
We whisper in your ear
Don't know if you're hearing clear
We work hard both day and night
To help you to do right, my dear

(Mesha)
We wouldn't know
What else to do
We love to work
Our intentions are true

(Kamali)
Feel free to live your life
We're along for the ride
Right by your side

(Chorus—All)
We're your angels
We'll help you go far
More real than wishes
You make upon the stars

We're your angels
A Celestial Heaven flight crew
We're part of the army of the man upstairs
We're angels, that's what we do

CHAPTER 3:
MORE THAN A FRIENDSHIP

Joe covered the distance between his house and Beth's in less than thirty seconds. He thought of how nice it was to have someone to hang around with that lived so close. Even though he had only been in Sweet River a few short weeks, he and Beth were practically inseparable.

"Hey, Beth. Do you think your mom will let us go to the river again today?" Joe stood outside the front door and called to Beth in the kitchen.

"I can't hear you very well. Just come in," Beth yelled.

Joe checked his old tattered sneakers for dirt and gingerly walked across the tan living room carpet. Since Steve didn't like to mop, Joe has been constantly reminded to remove his shoes before going in the house. Beth's mother never seemed to care if family or visitors removed their shoes. The Green home was inviting and friendly, with a bench on the front stoop, flowers that bloomed all summer in the flowerbeds, and the sound of piano music when Jill sat down to play for a few minutes each afternoon. There was always a smile on Bill and Jill's faces and a nice pat on the back for Joe. He felt accepted and he liked it.

As Joe peeked into the kitchen, he saw Beth standing in front of the stove. Steam was starting to rise from a large pot on the bright red burner. Joe didn't notice any odor of food cooking, which he thought was a little strange.

"What are you doing?" Joe asked.

"Oh, Mom and her crazy hummingbird feeders! We have probably fifteen of them, and they have to be filled a couple of times a week. Mom loves hummers," Beth explained.

"But what does that have to do with cooking? What are you making?"

"Hummingbirds drink sugar water from the feeders. That's their food. I have to mix sugar and water and heat it up a little bit so the sugar will dissolve. Can you help me get this off the stove?" Beth pointed to the large kettle.

"Sure. Do you always have to do this by yourself?" Joe asked.

"No, Mom usually does this, but she has been helping the lady down the street who broke her hip. Mom helps her with her therapy and takes her meals, cleans her house, whatever," said Beth.

"Your mom is a busy lady!"

The two of them carefully lifted the heavy pot out of the kitchen door to the backyard while avoiding a pile of shoes, miscellaneous tools, and a large rug. Once outside, Beth found a ladle and a funnel next to the shed. The sound of various birds filled the air, along with the buzzing of hummingbirds, which darted around the many feeders that lined the backyard. Joe stood and watched the tiny creatures in wonder as they darted about.

"They are crazy!" Joe exclaimed.

"Yeah. Hummers are my Mom's hobby, I guess," Beth explained. "She would feed them year round if she could, but it is best for the birds to migrate. See that one with the black head—with the little shiny purple patch on its neck?" Beth pointed to one of the many hummingbirds at the nearest feeder, which looked like a spaceship with large yellow flowers on it.

"Sure. There are lots of them," Joe said.

"That kind is pretty common around here. They are called black-chinned. I think my favorite are those green ones with the red neck. They are broad-tailed. Of course, the bright colored ones are the males."

"Like peacocks. They are the pretty ones," Joe remarked with a grin.

"Yeah. My mom's favorites are Allen's. They are really bright copper. They don't migrate around here though," Beth explained.

After they finished filling all of the feeders, they heard a door close. The garage door, which led to the backyard, opened, and Jill stepped out.

"Mom?" Beth yelled out just as the door opened.

"Hi. Yes, it's me. Just got a few groceries to put away. Poor Mrs. Jensen. I don't know if that hip will ever get better. Oh. Hi, Joe," Jill said with a little surprise as she saw him leaning against the wall of the shed.

"Hi, Mrs. Green. I came over to see if Beth and I could go to the river this afternoon. Would that be okay?"

"Did you get the feeders filled?" she asked Beth.

"Joe helped. We just finished."

"Then clean up the pot and you can go. Thanks for helping her, Joe. And please don't call me 'Mrs. Green.' Makes me sound kinda old." Jill laughed.

"Sorry."

"That's okay. Don't worry about it."

***

It didn't take Beth and Joe long to walk the mile to the river. They spent the afternoon finding creatures in the riverbank, swimming in the stream, and climbing on the branches of the tree that grew at the water's edge. One of the branches had an old rope swing tied to it. The rope was frayed and looked as if it would not support their weight, so they decided against trying it.

As they climbed the branch that extended over the edge of the river, Joe told Beth that he didn't like thinking that he might fall in and drown. He looked down cautiously into the murky water. He didn't want to appear afraid to his new and only friend in town, but something about the water frightened him. Beth just laughed and called him "a scaredy-cat."

Joe did not speak immediately after being teased by Beth. He continued to stare at the water. He remembered his many attempts to jump into swimming pools, creeks, rivers, and the ocean from a pier. No matter how hard he tried, he could not make himself do it. It seemed to bother him more the older he got. On this day, he wanted to prove to a girl that he could overcome his fear. His face still turned red each time he thought about crying in front of Beth the day they met. He felt especially determined to jump into the river with Beth watching; it would be his way of redeeming himself and perhaps gaining a little respect in her eyes—as well as his own.

"Okay, so I am gonna jump from this today," Joe finally declared, but there was hesitation in his voice. Beth was feeling a little guilty about teasing Joe. After all, they really didn't know each other very well, even though at times it felt as if they had been friends forever. Beth decided to encourage him.

"Well, sure you are. I know you can. Just forget about it. Don't think about it. Just jump. Like this." Beth pulled off her well-worn flip-flops, tossed them to the ground, and performed a perfect cannonball, making a large splash as she hit the water.

"See, silly!" Beth laughed and sputtered as she wiped water from her face. When she looked up at the tree, she saw that Joe's jaw was dropped in amazement. "It is easy," she yelled. "It isn't that high. Come on. I'll get out of the way. Just do it!"

Suddenly the sound of laughter and animated talking came from the gravel road that led to the river. A small group of boys jogged quickly to the edge of the river near the tree.

"Whatcha doing, Beth?"

"That looks like fun."

"Let's do it."

"I'm going in."

The chorus of comments and questions continued as three of the boys dropped their fishing poles, pulled off their shoes, and dove into the water. Two others climbed the big tree and moved past Joe in order to jump from the large branch. Their action caused Joe to make room for them by stepping closer to the trunk of the tree. As he leaned back onto the hard, rough wood, one of the boys noticed him.

"What's the matter?" said a boy with stringy black hair. "Ya scared?"

"No, just waiting my turn. That's all," Joe replied. He did not sound convincing.

Another boy stepped closer to Joe. "Come on. We'll jump together." He grabbed Joe by the arm and pulled him as he ran down the branch. Joe fought hard not to scream as he sailed through the air. Everything seemed to happen so quickly, yet in slow motion. Joe forgot to take in a deep breath before plunging into the river. His mouth and nose filled with water, forcing him to kick frantically toward the surface. Sputtering and coughing, he emerged. Joe continued to cough as he pulled himself out of the water and sat on the bank. One of his shoes was missing.

"That wasn't so bad, was it?" said the boy who had pulled him in. Beth and the boys gathered around Joe. Soon he was taking in normal breaths with only an occasional cough.

"No. That was just great," Joe lied. He knew better than to cry or get mad. He didn't want to look like a wimp.

Gathering himself, he stood and faced the boy. "My name is Joe. I'm new to Sweet River. I live near Beth." Beth was standing next to him and was not looking very happy.

"That was mean, Timothy. You didn't need to do that," Beth yelled.

"Oh, calm down, Beth. Tim didn't mean any harm." Tim's twin brother, James, always the peacemaker, reached his hand out to touch Beth's shoulder.

"Tell you what," Joe replied. "Let's do it again." Everyone's mouths opened in surprise and not a word was spoken until Joe had reached the tree and began climbing back up to the large branch. As he prepared to jump, he removed his remaining shoe and threw it to the ground.

"Are you sure? Where's your other shoe?" Beth asked as she followed him.

"Guess it's in the river. Maybe I'll be able to find it when I go back in." Leaning closer, Joe whispered. "Just so you know—I hate jumping into water. Scares the crap outta me."

Joe took a few deep breaths, held his nose, and jumped in feet first. Beth shook her head slowly and watched Joe disappear. She quickly followed after his head bobbed above the surface. They made their way to the shore and sat down on a large rock. As Joe looked down at his bare foot, Beth said, "Don't be too mad at Tim. He is okay, really."

James overheard the conversation. He turned to Timothy. "Maybe you should find his shoe." James pushed his brother toward the water.

"Quit it, James! What makes you so special and perfect? *You* find his shoe if you want." Timothy pushed James hard on the shoulder and ran toward the river with his brother following right behind. They proceeded to push and shove each other even after they were in the river.

Beth and Joe laughed as they watched the brothers pull each other's hair, ears, and noses in an attempt to win the fight.

"This happens all the time with them," Beth said. "But they are best friends the rest of the time. Maybe that's what we can be. You know, best friends, but without the fighting."

Joe smiled and said, "Well, maybe. I've never really had a best friend."

"Okay." Beth shrugged her shoulders slightly and smiled back.

***

They spent the rest of the afternoon practicing various ways to jump in the river, eating sandwiches the group had brought with them, and talking about the biggest fish in Sweet River. Earlier that spring, someone from out of state had heard about the infamous Grandpa Trout and was able to pull the twelve-pound fish to shore. The locals had been trying for years to catch it. The incident was a source of disappointment for many. Photos of the catch and the proud fisherman were printed in the local paper, and the original photo hung above the cash register at the mill.

Dusk arrived too soon, and the air temperature cooled, causing them to get goose bumps. Joe wondered how he would make it all the way home without his left shoe, but—more importantly— how he would explain it to his father. Tim and James walked over to where Joe was putting on his remaining shoe.

"Sorry about your shoe. No hard feelings, I hope," Tim said.

"Oh, it's okay. My dad is going to be pretty mad, though. I'll be working this off for a while. I hope he doesn't ground me."

"Here, take my shoes." James pulled his sneakers off and handed them to Joe.

"Oh, I can't take them! It's okay, really." Joe was genuinely surprised at the generous offer.

"Take them, Joe." Beth said. "Don't tell your dad that you lost yours. Just tell him you found another pair. I know—tell him you got them at a yard sale."

"Really? You think that would work?"

"They were getting too tight for me anyway," James replied. "Try them on."

"This is great! Thanks," Joe said as he tried them on. They were a perfect fit.

"We'd better get home." Tim turned to James, and the two of them gathered their fishing gear and headed toward the outskirts of Sweet River.

Tim turned back to Joe and said, "Hey. Next time, let's go diving at the quarry. I think you'd like it." With that, the twins started laughing. Beth chuckled a little and turned to Joe.

"That might not be such a good idea. You'll see why when you go there," Beth explained. "Let's get home before my mom sends the cops out for us."

Areanna

"That was a nice beginning to beautiful and lasting friendships. Everything went well, don't you think," Kamali asked. Joe's guardian angel was close at hand at the river to make sure that no serious harm came to Joe.

"Yes, but having most of this interaction planned made everything flow smoothly," added Mesha.

"One of Joe's lessons in this lifetime that he intended to work on was fear of water—especially jumping into it from even a short distance," Kamali explained. "He drowned in some other lifetimes. Joe was not too thrilled about being pushed in, but, as I said, it was part of the plan."

I added, "It is interesting to me to see how many fears are brought through from other incarnations. Beth has a few of those herself that she plans on addressing. We shall see how that goes."

Chapter 4:
Not an Ending or a Beginning

"Oh! I have slipped the surly bonds of earth and danced the skies on laughter-silvered wing. Sunward I've climbed and joined the tumbling mirth of sun-split clouds and done a hundred things you have not dreamed of—wheeled and soared and swung high in the sunlit silence. Hov'ring there, I've chased the shouting wind along and flung my eager craft through footless halls of air. Up, up the long, delirious, burning blue I've topped the windswept heights with easy grace where never lark or even eagle flew. And, while with silent lifting mind I've trod the high, untrespassed sanctity of space, put out my hand, and touched the face of God."

—John Gillespie Magee Jr.

"She was truly loved, and she will be sorely missed."

Beth didn't hear the microphone's final words even though the pulpit was directly in front of her. She had been occupying herself by pulling at hangnails and following the pattern of the flowers and leaves in her skirt, preferring to look down and avoid the pitiful gazes of the people around her. She never wanted to be the center of attention, especially now.

Bill sat stoically next to Beth. He was pale and shell-shocked as he pondered the reality that his wife of ten years was gone.

Bill and Jill had met while attending community college. Bill was studying management and Jill was in nursing school. A large group of students had gathered to watch a movie on one of the lawns on campus. They had arrived late and found themselves talking through the movie instead of watching. They had missed too much of the movie to follow the plot and Bill thought that the cute curly-haired young woman was much more interesting anyway. Jill found Bill's philosophy on education and life interesting and thought that it was funny that their names rhymed. Bill had a kindness about him, as well as being "drop-dead handsome." He reminded her of Paul Newman, but with green eyes instead of blue.

Bill's mind wandered through the memories of their dates, engagement, wedding, and early life together. They were thrilled when Beth came into their lives and were patient, doting parents. Now Jill was gone. Bill wondered how he would be able to raise Beth by himself—let alone live his life without Jill.

It had happened so quickly. There was no time to mentally or emotionally prepare for this. As quickly as the drunk driver plowed into her car, Jill's spirit left the earth—but not entirely.

Beth had been playing with her new best friend. They had developed quite a bond over the few months since their unforgettable meeting in the tree. Time meant nothing to them as they explored, talked, and experienced life in their neighborhood and in the wonderlands of the nearby river, junkyards, and forest.

This particular afternoon was progressing as usual. Jill spent the morning cooking breakfast for her daughter and husband. After Bill left for work, Jill cleaned the house, did some laundry, and made phone calls to ask for help with an upcoming bake sale.

She and Beth shared turkey sandwiches with Joe at lunchtime. Jill had a reputation for impromptu picnics, and this one was no exception. The meal included radish roses and mud pie pudding with gummy worms for dessert. They enjoyed the clear sky and the drone of hummingbirds in the backyard. After lunch, Beth and Joe left for the quarry. Beth had been promising to take Joe and Jill had finally relented. However, with that permission came a stern warning.

"There will be no jumping in, young lady! Now, be careful and have fun," Jill said. Then she added her familiar saying: "Love ya much." Beth gave her mother a quick kiss on the cheek, and the two kids took off out the door and down the street.

When the phone rang shortly after two o'clock, Jill gladly accepted a partial shift at the hospital for an ill co-worker. She could be there in a few minutes, but would only work until five o'clock. Bill would be home at that time, and they had plans to go shopping for lawn furniture.

Steve became the designated babysitter for the afternoon, volunteering for the task after Jill called and told him about the situation. It was Steve's day off from the mill, and he actually enjoyed the responsibility. The kids were usually good, didn't give him any trouble, and sometimes he would treat them to ice cream. He planned on taking them to Strikes & Burgers, his favorite place to eat. Steve thought that they made the best giant hamburgers he had ever eaten. It was fun for everyone to go there on karaoke night, watch black light bowling, and snack on French fries.

When Bill arrived home from work shortly after five, Jill's car wasn't in the driveway. He found her note on the kitchen table.

Bill. Will be home after five. Picked up a partial shift. Steve will get the kids from the quarry and bring them home after you and I get home from the store. Remember: lawn furniture. Love ya much.

Jill's heart at the bottom of the page—the same kind that she had put on every note to Bill since they had started dating—made Bill smile.

Suddenly, the quiet neighborhood silence was filled with the sound of sirens. In a small town like Sweet River, that piercing whine was not heard very often and got most people's attention. Residents found it hard to resist speculating what it meant, whether it was an accident or a fire. The volunteer EMTs responded to both, never knowing until they arrived at the fire station what they would be dealing with. Drivers would slow their vehicles down and parents would gather their children from the neighborhood streets quickly when the alarm sounded, giving the

EMTs a clearer and quicker drive to the fire station from their respective homes.

Their equipment and emergency vehicles were located at the fire station. They met there to find out from the dispatcher where the incident was and what they could be dealing with at the scene. While the chief made assignments, the team would gather additional equipment and medications and load the fire truck and ambulance. This would happen quickly; the crew had been working together for many years and was used to the routine. Their movements were robotic—even when they reached the scenes of accidents, illnesses, or structural fires. Later, they would allow themselves to decompress, share their emotions, and even cry. Their weekly practice scenarios helped them feel confident in their jobs.

Well, that can't be good, Bill thought. Suddenly, chills ran down his spine. Fear did that to a person—like cold water on a hot summer day. Bill tried to push his immediate thought away—that something had happened to Jill.

Bill walked briskly down the sidewalk, fear rising in his chest and strangling his throat. By the time he arrived at the Neal home, he was breathless.

"Hi, Steve. How are you today?" Bill attempted to speak normally through his rising fear. The effort caused a much higher pitch in his voice than he wanted.

"Hey. I'm good. How about you?" Steve noticed the strain in Bill's voice, but chose not to make anything of it.

"Did you hear the siren?" Bill asked.

"Don't know how anyone would miss that. Pretty loud, there must be a speaker close."

"Yeah. One of the volunteer EMTs lives on our street. Another one lives a couple of blocks away. The city placed the siren so they'd hear it if they were home. Where are the kids?" Bill asked.

Steve chuckled a little. "I just got back from checking on them at the quarry. That Joe is getting pretty good at jumping in the water. He was scared to death to jump in a wading pool until we moved here. I think Beth has helped him a bit. She ain't scared of anything."

"No, I think you are right there. She gets too gutsy for her own good sometimes," Bill said.

"Think I'll try Jill on the phone. She's not home yet. Thanks for watching the kids, Steve." Bill pulled his phone from his shirt pocket.

"No problem. I'll go get the kids in about an hour and feed them dinner—if that's okay with you. No reason to trouble Jill after working today. She probably won't want to cook, I'm guessing."

"Thanks. Just send Beth right home after dinner." Bill pushed the speed dial next to Jill's picture.

"Hi. This is Jill. I'm not available to speak to you right now. Please leave me a message. If you don't, that's okay. Have a great day anyway." The familiar tone on her voicemail was not comforting at the moment. Bill decided to do something he had never done before. He followed the sound of the ambulance that he could hear a short distance away. He knew that something was terribly wrong.

Coming upon the scene was something that would never leave Bill's memory. As upsetting as it is to see images of crushed automobiles in the newspaper or on television, having them right in front of your eyes is surreal and frightening. But this time the twisted metal was Jill's tan SUV. The hummingbird sticker that he had given her was in the back window.

Broken glass was scattered across both lanes of traffic. A passerby had stopped to help, but could not bring herself to leave her car when she saw the extent of damage. Other cars slowed as their drivers lowered their windows to get a better look. As Bill drove closer, he briefly saw a male driver slumped over the steering wheel of the other vehicle. The man was not moving. The impact of his car plowing into the left side of Jill's SUV had left an indentation that went almost entirely through the driver's seat. There were no skid marks to indicate he had even attempted to slow down. Bill pulled past the accident, found a clear place at the side of the road, and leaped out of his truck.

Bill's heart felt as if it was suddenly sinking and the strength in his knees left him. He ran as quickly as his shaking legs would carry him to where the EMTs were attempting to open the passenger door.

"Jill!" Bill yelled over and over again. With the window broken, Bill was able to reach his hand in and touch her face. It was abnormally cold and pale, with blood coursing down her left cheek. She did not respond to his voice. The EMT kept asking him to back up. It was as if Bill's head was in bucket with voices echoing around him. He could hardly make out the words—let alone what the message was.

"Sir, you've got to get out of the way. Please move now so we can help her."

Bill stumbled backward and watched as emergency personnel placed a cervical collar, looked at her eyes, checked her blood pressure, and applied a dressing to Jill's head. Bill could only watch helplessly. He paced back and forth over a six-foot piece of pavement—not more than twenty feet from the vehicle that held his unconscious wife.

Several minutes passed before they removed her carefully from the passenger side. Bill noticed a police officer covering the driver of the other vehicle with a sheet; his lifeless body occupied a stretcher near the fire truck. Bill felt no emotion at the time—not anger or sadness. He felt as if he were watching a movie. At the time he thought it was strange.

Others were arriving, and a crowd of people and vehicles maintained a respectable distance in order for emergency vehicles to get closer. Someone took Bill's arm and led him across the street. One of the local policemen came to Bill's side and saw his obvious distress.

"That's my wife! Is she going to be all right?" Bill pleaded.

"I don't know, but they will do their best." The policeman offered solace with a touch on Bill's shoulder. Bill had never felt so helpless and alone.

The EMTs pulled Jill from the vehicle and strapped her to a board. Bill ran forward as they started an IV and administered oxygen through a mask.

"Please, sir. She's in pretty bad shape and we need to hurry to the hospital."

"I'll drive you there," the policeman said. He escorted Bill to his cruiser and they followed the ambulance with sirens blaring.

***

At the hospital, an elderly volunteer escorted Bill to the family room. She wore a salmon-colored vest and white slacks. She, oddly enough, reminded Bill of his grandmother who had died when he was twelve. Her familiar smile and the brightness in her eyes made Bill feel calmer as she walked with him. For as many times as he had been at this hospital and thought he knew everyone there, Bill did not remember this woman. Bill was confused by the random thought that seemed to come from nowhere.

"I'll get you a glass of water," she said. She turned to walk back down the hall—and her movements had a vague familiarity.

Why would I think of Grandma Helen now? Strange. Bill's thoughts returned to the gravity of the situation. He took in a deep breath and looked around at the local artwork and photos on the wall, the plaques of remembrance of loved ones who had died, and pamphlets for local support groups. He could not make himself sit and paced between the couch and the coffee table until the volunteer returned with his water.

"You remind me so much of my grandmother," Bill said.

"That's nice. I bet she was a wonderful woman," she replied with a sweet, familiar smile.

"Yes, she was. She would have enjoyed this type of service that you do. Thanks for the water. It was very kind of you." Bill took a sip and placed the cup on the table. He had not realized how dry his mouth had become. The water tasted good, but he didn't think he could drink any more, given how tight his stomach felt.

Jill had been taken to the emergency department. The bustle of activity increased after a "Code Trauma" was called over the public address speakers. Employees from every department quickly assembled in the designated trauma room.

The doctor and several nurses worked in a frantic, but focused pace; each had a specialized task to perform. They placed monitors, listened to Jill's heart and lungs, opened sterile packs, and drew blood. It was not unusual for the staff to think of this bandaged person as a stranger because she had been identified as Jane Doe.

The police officer that brought Bill to the hospital walked into the trauma room to see how things were going.

The admission clerk asked, "Do you have her wallet or ID? Do you know who she is?"

"Yeah. I have her driver's license. Her name is Jill Green," the officer replied.

Everyone froze for a moment to absorb the information. Their pace picked up abruptly as they fought for the life of one of their own. Each of them had worked with Jill. Now they found themselves looking down at the broken body of someone they respected as a professional and loved as a friend.

Bill, alone in the family room, had been joined by a social worker who introduced herself as Sandy. She was there to take Bill to the emergency department to give him an update.

Sandy spoke quickly as they walked down the hall. "Jill's breathing is being assisted by a tube in her throat and there's a lot of equipment and people in the room. Her vital signs are being watched closely. I'll be standing by you if you need anything. I know this can be very frightening and I will be there," Sandy said reassuringly. She supported Bill's arm and opened the trauma room door.

As soon as they entered, he saw the stretcher in the center of the room. Monitors were blaring out their warnings about abnormal vital signs. Bill didn't really hear much of anything after that. He could not focus on conversations or activity. It was as if everything was being done and said in slow motion. In his mind, he repeated, "Save my wife. Save my Jill. Oh, God. Please don't take her from me."

Bill was assisted to a chair when Sandy saw that the color had drained from his face and he seemed to lose the strength in his legs. She held his hands and spoke, but Bill could not make out the words. He could only sit and watch helplessly as Jill's body could not sustain her life anymore.

It felt like an eternity, yet the moments passed quickly. It was as if time was playing a cruel trick on Bill. Too soon—yet not soon enough—he was asked if he wanted to be next to Jill, to talk to her and touch her. The monitors continued to notify the staff that something was not right, but Bill didn't need those messages to tell him that Jill was dying.

The doctor stood next to him. "We are assisting her breathing, but she has lost a lot of blood. She also sustained a severe blow to her head. We won't be able to transfer her quickly enough to a trauma center. All we can do is support her right now, but she won't last too much longer. I'm so sorry. We all love her."

Some of the staff sobbed and began to hug each other. Two of the nurses placed their hands lovingly on Jill's arm and leg while they looked across to Bill with sympathy and concern. All eyes were wet with tears.

Mustering his last bit of strength and determination, Bill cried out from the depths of his soul, "I can't believe this is happening. Jill! Fight, honey. Please—for me and Beth." He held her hand and looked at her face, willing her to open her eyes. Then, just as quickly, his energy was spent. He lowered his head and whispered into her ear, "Please, don't leave me. I love you so much."

The monitor above her head showed that her heart had stopped beating. There was only a flat line. Jill was gone.

***

Organ music played softly as Bill took Beth by the hand, leading her to the car that would take them to the cemetery. Bill thought over and over again that this was no place for a child and no place for his wife.

As he lovingly placed a red rose on her closed casket, a hummingbird came very close to him. He almost didn't even see it until it was within inches of his hand and the rose. He held perfectly still as it gently landed and then quickly flew away.

Chapter 5:
Part of the Plan

Areanna

"Do not worry, Jill. You are fine. Everything has been taken care of. Please trust me and follow me into the light. Everything will make sense once we arrive," Komsayah said softly and reassuringly.

Jill's disorientation caused her to question whether anything that was happening was real. She wondered whether she was dreaming, but this would be the most incredible dream ever—one that she would very much like to awaken from. She could hear familiar strains of a beautiful melody beckoning to her from all directions. The Lullaby filled her senses in every way and brought her a peace that was beyond joy. She was immersed in pure love.

As Jill struggled to make sense of what was happening, she focused her mind back to what did make sense: driving home from work. She remembered listening to the local news on the radio. She thought about the short shift at the hospital that had become a second home to her.

The nurses and doctors, as well as the other support staff,

made a good team. Their bonds of trust had grown through years of working side-by-side in a small hospital. They watched their children play soccer together, attended the same school programs, and sold cookies for fundraisers to buy gym equipment for the grade school. These dedicated people supported each other through labors and stitches, bad hair days and cooking disasters. They had come to know each other's tastes in fashion and taught each other how to knit and crochet.

Jill knew that she could trust the doctors and nurses—where one may not be as strong, another would step in without ego or criticism. That was what made this hospital a special place for her to work.

The Sweet River community readily supported the local hospital and its staff. Jill's picture had been in the weekly newspaper several times, educating the public on various diseases or health issues. She especially enjoyed the feeling of making a difference in public safety. Ironically, Jill had recently joined Mothers Against Drunk Drivers. A stack of flyers occupied the front passenger seat of her car.

It is amazing how many thoughts can go through your mind in such a short time, Jill thought. Just as quickly, another event came to her. It was as if she was living that moment again.

A flash of movement on her left took Jill's attention from the road ahead of her. *Why is that car traveling so fast? It isn't going to stop! Can't he see me?* Her thoughts were coming in a stream of questions that could not be answered by her alone.

What happened to me? What happened to the car? Why can't I remember?

Komsayah, standing to Jill's right and slightly ahead of her, continued to gently beckon her forward.

"Please, Jill. I will be able to explain more very soon." The voice sounded so peaceful and musical—in a way—and so familiar.

"No, I have to go back. This isn't right. I have to go back." Jill suddenly recognized the seriousness of her situation and her guide—her guardian angel.

"As you wish," Komsayah replied.

Jill immediately saw the familiar surroundings of the emergency room.

Who is that? They don't look very good, Jill thought.

"Why don't you look a little closer?" the melodious voice said. Jill leaned over the stretcher.

"Oh, no! It can't be! That isn't me—is it? Did that car hit me?" Komsayah's hands gently supported her soul. "Of course he did. He couldn't stop. He T-boned my car," Jill said under her breath in a slow, methodical way as her memory instantly returned.

Jill watched as the staff—her second family—frantically did all that they could to save her life. The monitor beeped loudly; the long tone indicated that Jill's earthly life was over.

"Oh, God. There's Bill." Jill immediately was at Bill's side, leaning in to rest her head on his shoulder. He completely ignored her efforts to touch him, to comfort him, and to get his attention. He could not hear her as she spoke to him.

"Bill. I'm right here. I'm okay. It's going to be okay. Please, Bill. Can't you hear me?"

Sadly, Jill turned to Komsayah. Jill's vision cleared even more and revealed spirits that she had known and loved forever. Her heart swelled as she recognized her soul family members, their guardian angels, and other guides. Jill's sense of peace and joy knew no bounds as she reconnected with each of them with a look and sharing of eternal love. The Lullaby was clear; its unmistakable melody reminded Jill of her connection with all.

This beautiful moment was interrupted by Komsayah's voice.

"Jill. It's time to go. You can come back and be with Bill and Beth later. You know that you can always be involved with them, in their thoughts and lives. But, now is the time to ..."

"Yes, I remember. Thank you, Komsayah, for everything you have done to help me in this lifetime. Thanks to all of you. I love you all so much. I am so grateful to be back and to remember everything. It seemed like so long ago that I came, but how quickly it passed. Time—what a crazy thing," Jill said with a little laugh. Even more heartfelt thoughts reached out to everyone and the communication of eternal love was felt completely.

Komsayah said, "Come, then. Let's go!"

The room was filled with a glorious, indescribable light that glowed from without and within each individual and melded together until all the individual lights became one.

I'm Free

I'm free
I have slipped out of the form
That was mine while I was there
Now I'm lighter than air

I'm free
Joyful with nothing to slow me down
I can soar
I'll find new worlds to explore

I think of you
I'm with you
Always with you

I'm free
The illusion of time passes by
We'll meet again
Share love and then
I'll find peace

I'm free
Love is forever and you'll feel me
In everything we are
Even the stars
That shine

I'm free

CHAPTER 6:
THE CLUB

And yet, as angels in some brighter dreams
Call to the soul when man doth sleep,
So some strange thoughts transcend our wonted themes,
And into glory peep.
—Henry Vaughan

"I now bring this club to order. Everyone, please listen as I have some announcements to make," Joe said with a little too much authority for the group of young friends. Chuckling or whispers came from everyone except James, who had not removed his earbuds and was bobbing his head to his music. Annoyed, Tim gave James a sharp elbow to the ribs.

"Hey, Joe. Don't be so serious," Tim said. He tossed a candy wrapper at Joe, which hit him on the arm.

"Yeah, I thought this was supposed to be fun." James's voice sounded like an echo of his brother's. At times it was difficult to tell them apart. Joe, after spending three summers swimming and playing with the twins, knew that Tim had a large mole on his

53

back that looked like a fish. If they were dressed the same or spoke on the phone, the brothers were almost impossible to tell apart.

"Okay. Sorry. I just want to find out something, that's all," said Joe. He sat down on the small, handmade stool the group had found while rummaging through the junkyard late at night. The others were seated on old mattress pads, a wooden chair without a back, and a lawn chair with a plastic pad. Joe asked, "Has anyone come up with a name for the club yet?"

Samantha (whom everyone called "Sammie") looked around the abandoned basement apartment. She had known about and had used this place to escape and hide when she was in trouble at home. This was the right time to share her hideaway with the friends she trusted the most. She had only moved to Sweet River two years earlier and, in many ways, had been treated like an outsider at school and in her neighborhood. Now she had finally found a group she felt comfortable with.

Sammie had literally turned heads when she walked down the hall on her first day at Sweet River Junior High. The tall blonde girl kept her blue eyes focused on the floor as she walked from her locker to class, never lifting her eyes to make contact with those who attempted to get her attention. She was pushed and shoved occasionally by girls who were jealous of her clear skin and thin body. It was hard for her to feel secure or trusting enough to make any kind of conversation with others.

Over time, Sammie had felt an increasing need for friends. Her home life—with a single, alcoholic mother—was difficult at best. Sammie's vivid dreams and premonitions were becoming stronger and more frequent. She wanted to share them with someone—anyone. She certainly could not talk to her mother about any of her experiences. Moving to a new town in order for her mother to clean offices and schools at night caused Sammie to be alone much of the time—even when her mother was not passed out on the couch with the television blaring. As she watched her classmates laugh and joke with each other, she became more and more determined to "break out of her shell" and make some friends, as her mother advised her.

One day, Sammie was eating lunch in the cafeteria. She took very little food to school; the refrigerator and cupboards at home were usually empty—except for her mother's alcohol and potato chips. Beth had been paired with Sammie for a writing assignment in English class. Beth had put off talking to her long enough. Sitting together for the first time, Beth immediately noticed Sammie's bruised apple and piece of bread.

"Not much of a lunch, I'd say. No wonder you are so skinny," Beth said.

Sammie dropped her head and picked at her fingernails. "I guess so," she replied quietly.

Beth touched Sammie's shoulder and said, "It's okay. Sometimes I wish I didn't like food so much. I came to talk to you about our assignment for Ms. Lee's class."

"Okay. I guess we should get busy with it."

As Beth and Sammie worked on the short story at lunch over the next few days, Beth came to see Sammie as extremely shy and unsure of herself. Beth invited her over to her house often to work on the assignment. Sammie never invited Beth to her home, and Beth didn't push it—even though she was very curious about

Sammie's mother. Beth missed her own mother very much and was a little jealous at times of those who had mothers.

As their friendship grew, Beth and Sammie shared makeup and clothes. Sammie eventually trusted Beth enough to share her vivid—and sometimes disturbing—dreams. Beth eventually convinced Sammie to join Beth's group of friends for movies and bike riding. Everyone eventually accepted and grew to appreciate Sammie for her loyalty. She never spoke badly of anyone and always found positive things to say about everyone—even the teachers that most kids did not like.

At the club, she was with those she trusted the most in the world. Sammie spoke quietly and thoughtfully, as if the idea was forming in her mind and it wasn't quite ready to make itself known. "What are the things that we share the most? What really makes us special or different from other kids at school? Maybe the name could be something like that," she suggested.

"Well, we aren't the smartest kids in school," James observed. "We aren't all even in the same grade."

"I don't think that matters," Joe replied. "Do you have any ideas, Beth?"

"No, not really. I'm not sure why I'm even here in the first place—other than you invited me," Beth said to Joe. "You talk about space all the time. You draw pictures of things that don't even look like people, like creatures from space. And Wyatt can't stop making buildings."

All eyes turned to the small teenager on the floor sitting quietly with various blocks he had produced from his backpack. He had already built a house with them on the dusty floor. Hearing his name, Wyatt looked up from his construction.

"So, I like to build stuff. Anything wrong with that?" Wyatt asked.

Joe said, "No, but I've never seen a house like that before. It's cool."

"Thanks." With that remark, Wyatt knocked down the walls of his creation and gathered the blocks together in a pile.

Wyatt was small for his age, but he was a feisty, active child. He came from one of the poorest families in town and never had any new clothes, but he was top in most of his classes. Even as a young child, he loved to build things and became very creative in the items he used. He escaped into his own creations when he started putting together sticks, broken glass, small boards, or plastic. Being teased for his art, his size, or his unkempt appearance did not seem to bother him. Eventually, the bullies left him alone since they could not seem to break him down.

Being the youngest of eight in his family was difficult. He literally had to fight at times to get enough to eat, and his parents seemed to be too busy with the others to help him. Wyatt had learned to take care of himself when he was young from watching others and reading. He loved to read—especially anything that had to do with construction or mathematics. He worked hard for his teachers, and they appreciated him for it. Most of them were willing to extend extra help to him, and he blossomed because of it.

Wyatt and the twins became friends in shop class. The twins struggled to cut pieces of wood or use the equipment correctly.

Wyatt stepped in time and time again to help them. Eventually they started spending more time outside of school together.

Beth turned to look at Sammie. "You talk about your crazy dreams—and sometimes stuff happens when you touch people. Tim thinks he can read animals' minds, and James is way into music. I'm into being outdoors, watching the clouds, and swimming in the river. You know—normal stuff. I don't think we like anything the same. Besides, I think all of you guys are kinda weird." A big smile came over Beth's face and she said, "But you are my friends."

No one took offense at Beth's remarks, and the group looked around at each other. In their eyes shine genuine kindness and understanding. Each one felt a kinship with the others.

Sammie said, "Well, I don't want to call us "The Weirdos." Everyone laughed.

"I've been working on a school report about Native Americans and totems. What if that was the name of the club?" Tim asked. "We are all different like the animals in a totem pole."

Joe said, "I like it. The Totem Club."

Sammie nodded her head in agreement. "We could even learn about an animal we like and make a totem with them," she said.

"That would be cool," Beth said. "I could bring knives for everyone to carve with. You know, I'm pretty good with a knife."

"Yeah, I know. I have a scar to prove it," Joe said as he pointed to his butt.

Beth's mouth opened in surprise, but suddenly snapped shut.

She squinted her eyes at Joe and said defensively, "Not everyone has to know about that." Joe just laughed.

"Okay, so maybe your knife skills have improved since then. No worries," Joe said.

Wyatt said, "Well, that's it, then. We are officially 'The Totem Club.' Now to figure out which animal I want to be. Hmm."

"Yours should be something that likes to build—like a beaver," Beth said.

Tim explained, "According to the legends, a totem animal finds you, you don't necessarily pick it yourself. If you don't know right now, maybe before we have our next meeting, we can pay attention and our animal will find us."

Joe said, "That seems like a good idea. So now that we have a name for the club, does anyone have anything weird that happened to them that you want to talk about?" They sat in silence for what seemed like a very long time. Each one of them was lost in their thoughts, wondering what they thought they could share about their experiences. They did not want to be made fun of. They had all received plenty of ribbing and ridicule—some of them from the time they were very small. Even teachers laughed at them or told them that they were crazy when they shared what they had seen or heard. At times, they even questioned the things that had happened to them—not always sure whether they were real. But here, with the Totem Club, they had a sense that they could be open in ways they had not been before.

"I had a dream the other night that was pretty scary," Sammie started. "Is that what you mean, Joe? Do you want me to talk about my dream?"

"Sure," Joe said. "Maybe then it won't seem so scary."

"It seemed so real. It was very clear. And it seemed like it was me, but it wasn't. You know what I mean." Several shook their heads in agreement. "I was walking through a field, and everything was dry and kinda brown. The sun was shining, and it was warm. I don't ever remember going through a place like that, but it was nice. The plants and trees were just like the ones that grow around here." Sammie stopped for a moment as she revisited the dream in her mind.

"Then I came to a cliff. It wasn't too high, and there was a small lake at the bottom of the cliff. It wasn't really a lake because it was lined with big square boulders, like they'd been cut that way."

"Sounds like the quarry," Tim said. "We've been there swimming lots of times. We dive from the edge. It's fun."

"Well, I've never been there so I don't know if that is it or not. In the dream, I felt like I wanted to jump, but the water didn't look deep enough. I felt like if I jumped, I would hit a rock or something." Sammie ran her fingers through her long, blonde hair.

As Joe listened, it was as if he could see the scene playing out in his head. It seemed so real to him that he actually closed his eyes and imagined himself walking down a dusty path toward the quarry.

"I remember that there were others there—not strangers. I'm not sure who they were. We were having fun. It was like we were seeing each other again after a long time. That was the feeling I got." Sammie took a long breath and went on.

"This is where I remembered being afraid to jump, but talking myself into it. Someone was yelling at me from the lake, telling me not to, but I ignored them. When I jumped, it was like I was floating in air for a long time, and I thought about how I'd been so afraid before. Not just this time, but other times I had been afraid. And I was glad that I wasn't afraid anymore."

Everyone listened closely to every word Sammie spoke. Each one was caught up in the scene and the emotions, but Joe had chills through his entire body. He shivered so abruptly that Beth noticed his movement and shot him a puzzled look. Joe took a deep breath, looked at Beth, and gave her a weak smile. Beth thought that he looked a little pale and wondered whether he was getting sick.

"Before I hit the water, I knew just what to do. I knew I had to dive in a special way to avoid the rocks at the bottom, but something went wrong. As soon as I went under the water, there was a big rock and I was going right for it. I couldn't move fast enough to stop from hitting my head on it. I knew I was going to drown."

Sammie's voice changed as she remembered her feelings from the night of the dream. It still felt real and her emotions were close to the surface. Joe's hands clenched in fists by his side and held his breath.

"I woke up right then and was gasping like I was drowning. I knew I wasn't, but I was choking so much it woke my mother up." Sammie took another deep breath and looked around. "That was it. What do you think?"

"I think that was a crazy dream," Tim said.

"Oh, I know it's just a dream. Sometimes they are scary, but they aren't real," Beth said with conviction. She had heard Sammie describe a few of her dreams and had actually seen them come true, but Beth didn't want to believe this one for some reason. It felt very real and frightening to her. She just wanted to get out of there and shake off the feeling she was having. "I've got to get home. I don't want my dad to find out I'm in this creepy place talking about silly dreams. Hope you guys have fun with your new club."

"Aw, come on, Beth. You don't have to go, do you?" Joe asked.

"Yeah. I'm going home. I'll see you all tomorrow at school." Beth opened the creaky door and walked down the fire escape.

"I can stay longer," Wyatt said. Turning to Tim, he asked, "Do you have any books about totems? Beth thought I should be pick a beaver, but I don't know."

"Sure, I can show you some articles I found on the Internet," Tim answered.

James quietly asked Sammie, "Are you okay?"

"Sure. I'm fine," she answered in an attempt to convince herself that she would be eventually.

"Can we all meet next week?" Joe asked the group.

After a consensus, everyone gathered their books and belongings and descended the rickety stairway.

Areanna

"It will be nice to see how Wyatt responds to your influence and energy, Mr. Wright. Do you feel that the world is ready for another revolutionary architect?" I asked the spirit standing next to the young teenager crouched on the floor with the blocks.

Sarah had accompanied me to this gathering and found the whole thing fascinating. Some of the spirits assembled were familiar to her, and the energy in the room was exciting and uplifting. She whispered to me, "I love this part, watching how everyone responds to the influences on them. It is interesting to find how some souls respond more than others."

"He seems promising—and please call me Frank. We've known each other too long to use formality." Frank Lloyd Wright had been an interesting and cooperative soul to work with through several "projects" on Earth. He enjoyed seeing his influence blossom into beautiful—and interesting—creations.

"Well, Joe certainly has been listening and paying attention in this lifetime—that's for sure." Carl Sagan appeared and walked toward the group assembled in the abandoned apartment. Of course, none of the embodied souls of the Totem Club knew that the spirits were there. "He is truly fascinated by space—almost as much as I was at that age." He laughed heartily and added, "Well, maybe not *that* much."

"Happy you could join us, Carl, as always," I said.

"My pleasure." Turning to his left, Carl said, "Henry. It is very nice to see you here. How does it feel to work with someone on Earth again?"

"Oh, I enjoy the escapade and the dreams. These incarnated souls on Earth at this time generally seem to take life pretty seriously—so I will keep my influence interesting for her.

Samantha was responsive from a very young age. Since we worked together in other lifetimes, she may feel a sense of déjà vu," Henry Vaughan replied.

Frank rejoined the conversation. "Oh, that's right. That was a couple of centuries ago, wasn't it?"

"Yes," answered Henry. "Samantha wrote poetry then. We have decided to work on philosophy this time—along with vivid dreams and predictions. She won't realize much of this for a while."

I couldn't help but comment on the soft, glowing cloud of swirling color that surrounded Beth. I said, "It is always fascinating to me to see the influence of Gaia—as well as feeling her loving presence. Those who sense the sacredness of Mother Earth are blessed, and I can see that Beth feels very comfortable when she communes with nature."

There was a band of specialized angels surrounding the Gaia energy that enveloped Beth's physical being. The Lullaby could be heard from their heavenly voices, and many members of the group hummed or sang the familiar restrain.

"Anamosa, you must feel particularly close to this energy—after being in the Sauk tribe," Carl said.

"Yes, that is true. In my last incarnation, I learned much from the land: growing vegetables, hunting, fishing, and enjoying the big lake the tribe lived near. Tim wanted to spend this lifetime enjoying some of those things, but also to gain a sense of peace with the land," Anamosa replied. "He has the potential to be a great influence in the conservation movement in his country."

"And, to round out this group, we have Masit Khan. How are you contributing to the world of music through James?" I asked.

Masit Khan had enjoyed listening quietly to the group interactions, taking an observant posture. His being had a beautiful smile and a twinkle in his eyes. "My essence is influencing James to learn about music, to learn to play an instrument, and to possibly create music of his own. He is very creative in his own mind about music composition and does not limit his preferences to Western music. Because of my contribution to the world with regards to the sitar, James may be attracted to the guitar, but we shall see. He is thinking about asking for one for his next birthday."

"We all agree that music is an important influence in the world. We thank you for what you have done and are continuing to do, Masit," Frank added.

We continued to enjoy the last of the Totem Club's meeting, and then dispersed along with them to their various homes.

Sarah and I talked more about the interactions and she said, "I sure hope that I am open to the influences I have chosen this time. I hope I am able to remember more of what I am going to learn and how I can grow this time on Earth."

I answered, "The potential is there for everyone to grow spiritually and intellectually if they will but allow their path to open to them. Your soul family members have chosen well, but we know that they may or may not be open all the time. That is perfectly fine. All is in perfect order."

CHAPTER 7:
WAS IT REAL?

Joe stared out the window, watching the snowflakes dance and drift in the air, slowly descending onto the cars in the nearby parking lot. He wondered if winter was ever going to end—and it was only the first part of December. Only a few years had passed since he and his father had moved to Sweet River, but it felt like a lifetime since it had been warm and he was enjoying himself with friends at the river.

"Mr. Neal. Would you like to come back and join us in this discussion?" Mr. Thomas's voice broke through the Joe's reoccurring daydream—the one where he was running through the woods toward a cliff, and then diving from the top of a waterfall into a large pool. When he wasn't having that particular daydream, the other one that occupied his mind had him zooming through the night sky toward Orion.

"Sure," Joe said. Several junior classmates chuckled. Joe did not seem particularly embarrassed.

"Why do you think ghosts were so important in *A Christmas Carol?*" Mr. Thomas asked.

This was one of Joe and his father's favorite stories. They had made a tradition of reading it every Christmas season since Joe was very young. He smiled as he remembered talking about the ghosts in the story. "Ghosts could see the whole picture of what had happened and what could happen. Maybe the ghosts were the only thing that would get Scrooge's attention," Joe answered.

"Okay. I would agree. But many people don't believe in ghosts. Do you think Scrooge was just dreaming and that the ghosts were just part of his dream? What do you think, Beth?" Mr. Thomas took a step in Beth's direction.

Beth answered quietly, "I believe in ghosts, so I think Scrooge really saw them."

Several people in the classroom started to laugh. Beth's mood turned to anger. "Well, what do you know, anyway?" She spoke to the group of girls seated immediately behind her. It was not unusual for these particular girls to laugh and make fun of Beth. They would make remarks about her clothing, her interests, and her "boyfriend Joe."

"All right. All right." Mr. Thomas brought some order to the class with his authoritative voice. "Let's get back to what we were talking about."

***

After school, Joe and Beth met at her locker. Beth seemed upset as she rummaged through the contents at the bottom. Upon finding a piece of gum, Beth put it in her mouth before turning to face Joe.

"Why would you say that in class—about believing in ghosts,

I mean?" Joe was hoping that Beth would decide to explain herself; opening herself up to him might dissipate her black mood.

"Oh, I'm not sure I believe what happened myself. It was probably nothing." Beth was reluctant to saying too much—she did *not* want Joe to think she was crazy. They had been best friends for years, but there still were some things that she didn't exactly want to share with him. This was one of those things. Beth shut her locker with more force than necessary, drawing attention from the other students in the hall.

"Come on. I won't laugh. Don't you trust me?" His words stung Beth a little.

"Okay. But you've got to promise me that you won't say anything to anyone," Beth said.

"Okay," Joe said slowly. The two of them walked silently through the main doors of the school and across the street to a small park.

Beth sat down on a damp park swing. The snowstorm from earlier in the afternoon had left everything wet and shiny, but no snow remained. Joe adjusted his backpack and sat on the adjoining swing. He began to sway back and forth slightly and a protesting squeak came from the swing.

Beth took a deep breath and started speaking.

"It wasn't long after the accident." Beth referred to her mother's death as "the accident." It was still too painful to call it anything else.

"I had just gone to bed, and my dad was in the living room watching the news. I heard him turn off the TV, go to his bedroom, and shut the door." Beth seemed to be struggling with the words to explain what she experienced next.

"I had closed my eyes and was thinking how much I missed my mom." There was a slight catch in her voice and Beth took another deep breath. "I felt something touch my arm—like someone was petting it. I wasn't sure what was going on, so I kept my eyes closed. Then it felt like something heavy was set on the bottom of my bed. I thought that maybe my dad had come in my room to check on me or something. I opened my eyes and was going to say something to him, but my mom was sitting there." Beth looked toward the top of the trees as she remembered the smell of roses, the smile on her mother's face, and the peace she felt when she saw her image.

"I thought I was dreaming. I couldn't believe my eyes. My mom was there—smiling at me. I thought if I said something she'd disappear, so I didn't dare say anything out loud. I could hear her voice in my head. She told me that she loved me and would always be near. She told me not to be sad and that everything was going to be all right. Then she just disappeared." Tears spilled down over Beth's red cheeks. She sniffed loudly and wiped her nose on her sleeve.

Joe didn't know what to do or say. He had never heard Beth mention that she had seen the ghost of her mother, so the surprise he felt left him speechless. He had learned that the best way to handle her when she was sad was to simply put his arm around her shoulder. Neither one of them spoke for what felt like a very long time.

Joe said simply, "Wow. I'm surprised you hadn't told me this by now. Did you think I would laugh at you or make fun of it?"

"No. Oh, I don't know. It felt so real, and I thought that talking about it would make it sound fake or something." Beth sighed deeply and said, "I just wanted it to happen again, but it never has. Do you think she really is around like she said?"

The sound of a crow brought their thoughts back to the park and the realization that it was getting colder and darker.

"Maybe we'd better get home. I don't want my dad to send the cops out for us," Joe said.

Beth wiped her nose and eyes again, straightened up in the swing and turned to look at Joe.

"Do you think I'm crazy?" Beth asked.

"No, not really. I think it was real," Joe said with unusual maturity.

"Good. Now, don't you tell anybody about this, okay?" Beth's serious look caused Joe to smile.

"No problem. Let's get home," he said as he took her hand and they walked in the peaceful late afternoon. Both were silently caught up in their own thoughts about life, death, ghosts, and what happens to someone after they die. More questions than answers filled their minds, but it didn't seem like the right time or the place to discuss them.

Areanna

As Beth and Joe approached their respective homes after waving good-bye, the unseen group accompanying them broke the silence.

"I remember wondering what Beth was thinking when I visited her that night. Her thoughts immediately came to me, but I wasn't sure my thoughts were getting to her," Jill said quietly to Komsayah. "Now I know she did hear me. That makes me very happy."

"I am sure, in time, your visits will be a comfort to her as well," said Komsayah. "Bill may be able to hear or sense you, too."

"I've tried several ways to get his attention. The first thing he seemed to notice was the hummingbird at the cemetery. I thought that would be a nice reminder to him that I was around, considering how much value I placed on those cute little birds," Jill said.

"We would all like to see Bill wake up a little more. But, remember, it is his choosing and timing," said Nochintac as teal and a glorious golden bronze infused the mist of pale pink. Nochintac was a magnificent angel, appearing currently as a loving being of Native American heritage. This type of energy spoke to Bill's spirit in many lifetimes and Nochintac was pleased to serve and assist Bill with that particular essence.

"This is a major lesson for him and was of his choosing. Remember that it was planned and you have done well, Jill. He knows that you love him."

"Yes, I know. It's just that communicating with him through forgetfulness and fear has its challenges. I would prefer that he remember me in love and not sadness so much."

"I understand," said Nochintac. "I am with him and sense at

times that he is comforted by me and others. There are those who can assist us in sharing love from this realm."

"Of course." Komsayah smiled warmly. "We will never stop being a presence in the lives of those in sorrow and pain."

CHAPTER 8:
THE TRICKS OF REALITY

"The reality of the other person lies not in what he reveals to you, but what he cannot reveal to you. Therefore, if you would understand him, listen not to what he says, but rather to what he does not say."
—Kahlil Gibran

"Beth, watch. Are you watching? Beth?" Joe's voice carried more annoyance with each word that he spoke. Ever since the magic shop opened in Sweet River, Joe had become increasingly interested in the art of illusion. Beth knew that it was all a trick, but played along—at least most of the time.

"Sure, sure. I'm watching." Beth turned toward Joe and away from a passing red car. She wondered if she'd ever get to drive anything so nice.

She had been staring out of the window of Strikes & Burgers, hoping to see something that would be more exciting outside than the inside of the 1950s-style burger joint. Beth had read every metal poster on the wall with the tractor logos, bowling pins, hamburgers, and milkshakes in the two years that she had worked here. Nothing had really changed much in the décor since Beth's family had been dining here—along with everyone else in town—since it had opened fifteen years earlier. The black and white checkerboard floor still matched the wallpaper border surrounding the room, and the red vinyl barstools had only been recovered once.

It had been a particularly boring shift for Beth. There had been only two parties all afternoon; the bowlers only wanted drinks and fries. The cook was outside at a picnic table, reading the sports section. Beth knew where to find him if any customers came in.

"Okay. Take the deck of cards and shuffle it." Beth did as she was instructed. Joe said, "Now, pick a card out of the deck, memorize which one it is, and place it on the bottom of the deck."

Beth chose the two of hearts and placed it on the bottom of the deck. She handed the deck back to Joe and he slipped the entire deck into the empty box.

"Now, I'll bet I can read your mind and tell you what card you picked." Joe spoke as if he was speaking to a crowd. He twisted the box over and over in his hands and finally held it close to his forehead as if the answer would magically enter his brain.

"Okay, smarty. What card was it?" Beth's patience was wearing thin. She just wanted to get home, change out of her work uniform—an old cheerleading outfit—and relax by the river.

"The two of hearts. Ladies and gentlemen, you may hold your applause," Joe said quietly. He smiled wryly and winked.

"How did you know?" Beth sounded a little surprised.

"Trade secret. I can't tell you or maybe you could just pay me for the answer. I can be bought, you know," Joe joked.

"Ha. Ha. Very funny. Can we please go home now? My feet are killing me in these shoes," Beth's white and black bowling shoes had a splattering of catsup over her right foot. She could not get used to the smell of old cooking grease from the deep fryer that clung to her clothes and hair.

"Sure. Let's go." Joe gathered his latest magic trick and his schoolbooks as he gulped down the last of his chocolate shake. Having his girlfriend work at the best fast food place in Sweet River had its advantages, he thought.

As many times as Joe tried to get Beth to talk about seeing her mother's ghost, it was like hitting his head against a brick wall. Beth would either change the subject or pooh-pooh the topic. Once she even accused him of trying to cause a fight that would break them up. Joe simply wanted to understand more about how Beth felt about life and death, but she would not discuss it. Lately his deeper thoughts involved the world of space and what would be defined as "real." Maybe she was ready to finally listen to him.

"Have you ever wondered about life on Earth? Is there a reason for us? Did we evolve from apes? What is the soul? I mean, have you ever *really* thought about it?" Joe asked.

"What do you mean? Like the stuff churches ask? Why are we here? Where did we come from and where are we going after we die? That kind of stuff?" Beth wondered how deep this conversation would go. She was not in the mood to put any mental energy into it.

"Well, sort of. We've never really talked about it much, but I want to know what you think. Really." Joe's voice had a strange sincerity that it normally did not have.

"Oh, great! Are you getting all philosophical on me now, Joe? You know I don't like talking about it."

"Okay, we don't have to talk about it. I just wondered what you thought, that's all. I just wish you'd open up a little more about it."

"Sorry. I didn't mean to make you mad." Beth touched his arm gently. "Go ahead, tell me what you mean."

Joe took in a deep breath. "Do you remember when we went to watch the meteor shower last summer?"

"Sure. That was pretty cool," Beth said.

"Well, it got me thinking about what is really out there. You know, in space—past the stars. I don't mean the kind of stuff like Martians or spacemen, but what really made it all. There's lots of planets and stars and galaxies we can't even imagine. Maybe there are other places kind of like Earth." Joe stopped walking and turned to Beth. "What do you think?"

"You've talked about some of this stuff before. I know you have been interested in space travel and all that since you were a kid. So is this more than that?" Beth stopped to look Joe in the eyes. She wanted to be able to see his face when he answered her question.

"Yeah, sure. Don't you ever wonder about how stars were made in the first place? How everything got where it is right now?

If there are others like us wondering about the same thing?" Joe hoped that Beth shared the same wonderment and amazement in the night sky, but he was doubtful. He felt as if a floodgate had opened and he wasn't willing to close it quite yet. He looked sincerely at her. "I want to know what you believe, Beth."

"In church, they tell us that God created all of this, so if there is any more life out there in space, then I guess God would have created it, too. 'Worlds without number' the scriptures say." Beth raised both arms in the air in a grand fashion. "I don't think I need to know anything more than that. I trust the scriptures and what I hear at church. They know more than I do."

"Okay, so you haven't thought for yourself about that kind of stuff? Do you trust everything you read? History seems to change when science or somebody discovers something different. I can't just buy into what others think they know from books that change over time."

Beth scowled, causing a deep furrow between her brows. "You mean to tell me that you don't believe in the Bible?" She was truly dumbfounded by what she was hearing.

Joe realized the seriousness of what Beth believed and attempted to avoid an argument. "Sure, there's probably stuff that really happened in the Bible. It's just that I think about other ideas and movies like *The Matrix*, too. I've wondered if it's all just like a magic act, like everything really doesn't exist." Joe hoped that he was making his point without causing her to react negatively.

"What in the world are you talking about? That's crazy! I'm real, you are real, the trees are real, the sky is real. I couldn't feel you if you weren't real." She poked him in the ribs—hard.

Joe started walking, rubbing his left side. He still felt as if he had a point to make. "Yeah, I know. But maybe this stuff just seems real and we are just dreaming or like in a play or something. What if God wanted us to think this was real, but He was just hiding behind a screen or something, like in the Wizard of Oz?"

"Pay no attention to the man behind the curtain! He's just God messing with you," Beth said sarcastically. "Who have you been talking to? What gave you these ideas?"

"Nobody did. Never mind. Forget about it. This is going nowhere."

"Why don't you come to church with me and Dad on Sunday? You might learn something. The people there are very nice. What do you think?"

The silence felt like a heavy, dark blanket.

"No, thanks. I'm good. Gotta go. See ya tomorrow." With a quick turn, Joe walked briskly to his house. Beth watched as he reached his mailbox. They looked at each other, bid each other a perfunctory wave, and walked through their respective front doors.

Areanna

"Beth gave Joe a little run for his money, didn't she?" Mesha's infectious smile brought added joy to the group of angels observing the discussion between the two teenagers.

Kamali started chuckling. "Joe enjoys the challenge of sharing his thoughts with someone with opposing views in order to test his ideas and thoughts—to hear them spoken aloud and see how that feels. Beth is playing her part well."

"We know this won't be the last of their talks about the reality of life, the dogma of organized religion, the influence of movies, and the like. It is nice to see how their relationship has grown over the past few years. They have trust in each other as dear friends, which is an important part of a long-term relationship." Mesha moved a little closer to Beth's ear and whispered, "Beth, open your heart and mind just a little more to what Joe is saying. He has a point, my dear."

"Oh, if only that type of persuasion worked every time," said Kamali. "Our jobs would be much easier."

"But no less joyful or satisfying," Mesha added. "I understand that you have been working with Joe more in his dreams. Has he been receptive to that?"

"Yes, it seems so. He is having more dreams about flying through space, visiting other planets and star systems, but his recall has not improved at this point. It is fine, though. He has been checking out books at the library and looking up information on the Internet."

CHAPTER 9:
GOING THEIR SEPARATE WAYS

*"When I was a child I spake as a child I understood
as a child I thought as a child, but when I
became a man, I put away childish things."*
—1 Corinthians 13:11

Friends and families gather in similar observances across the country to watch high school seniors shake someone's hand and receive a piece of paper. The simple—yet symbolic—rite of passage into adulthood is a tradition that doesn't seem to die, even though many are receiving their diplomas in other ways without the pomp and ceremony. After graduation, the senior class of Sweet River High would return the next day to sign yearbooks, say their good-byes, and start on their own separate journeys.

"I never thought we'd get these kids this far," Steve said to Bill as they waited for their children to walk across a stage on the football field. "We didn't do too bad, did we?"

"Nope, we didn't," Bill agreed. "I just wish there was a way that Joe and Beth could continue with some kind of education.

They're smart and could do well in the world. I think they are just worried about us. And, to be honest with you, I would really miss them if they decided to go anywhere."

Neither of their kids had received scholarships—not even to the nearest community college, which was two hours away. They told their fathers that they would look into taking online courses, but Steve and Bill did not believe that this would happen any time soon. Bill had gotten Joe a part-time job at the mill for the summer and Beth would continue to work full-time at Strikes & Burgers.

"Well, maybe something will come up. I have a feeling they won't be here forever, even though right now the only thing they seem to think about is being together. I can't believe how close they've been through the years. Beth's a great gal. She has always felt like a daughter to me." Steve's voice cracked and his eyes became moist with tears. Despite his large frame and tough exterior, Steve had a very soft heart.

All Bill could do was nod his head in agreement. His own emotions were right under the surface, but he could openly cry without shame. Crying would release some of the pain he felt in his heart after Jill's death, but the wound was deep.

As he listened to Steve, Bill thought about the many times he missed Jill while raising Beth alone. He remembered the questions Beth had about the changes her body was going though, the mother-daughter activities he attended at the church with her, and the shopping trips for makeup and hair products. It was the day-to-day things that a mother should be a part of, but—for nine years—Bill had been both mother and father.

"Fredrick Flint." The name brought a loud cry of "Stoner" from the group two rows behind Bill and Steve, which brought them out of their respective thoughts.

"Here comes Beth," Bill said as he nudged Steve. They straightened in their seats, grabbed their cameras, and started shooting photos and a video. Bill had to wipe his eyes quickly and take a deep breath in order to hold the camera still. Then he saw Beth clearly through the lens.

"Elizabeth Green," the announcer called. Beth walked proudly across the stage with her head held high, looking as if she were floating in her red graduation gown. Steve started whistling loudly, and Beth gave a small wave in his direction. She did not want to make eye contact with anyone, as she felt she would start crying at any moment. As happy as she was to be finished with high school, she missed her mother very much. She shook the superintendent's hand and reached for her diploma as the principal handed it to her. When she turned to look up at Bill, she threw him a kiss before walking down the stairs.

Instead of returning to her seat, Beth lifted her gown and ran behind the bleachers to the area where the remaining graduates were gathered. She quickly found Joe, and they produced a straitjacket from a large bag tucked behind a false curtain.

"Hurry!" Joe said as he struggled to get in the jacket. Beth quickly grabbed several padlocks and asked those standing around to help her buckle the leather straps and attach the locks to the back of the jacket. Wyatt pinned a sign that said "Sweet River High" on the back, and the look was complete.

"This is so crazy!" Tim shook his head from side to side. "It's great!"

"I hope you don't get kicked off the stage," James said as Sammie frantically asked the crowd to be quiet. The Totem Club had been planning their stunt for weeks, and they thought it would be a fitting symbol of getting out of high school.

"I gotta go. I'm next. Good luck, Joe," Sammie called as she quickly went to the head of the line.

"I'd better go take my seat before someone comes looking for me," Beth said as she gave Joe a quick kiss on the cheek. "I'll take lots of pictures."

"Good. Now hurry." The line of students parted for Joe to take his place.

Finally it was Joe's turn to walk up the stairs and across the stage. His appearance drew gasps and laughter from the crowd. Many camera flashes went off as Joe leisurely walked toward the superintendant. The superintendant's jaw dropped and he automatically lifted his hand to shake Joe's—as he had with all the other students. Joe made eye contact with him and then looked down at his extended hand as Joe shrugged his shoulders. The superintendant started laughing, patted Joe on the shoulder, and said, "Carry on, Mr. Neal."

The principal did not take the joke as well and raised his voice slightly. "That's enough, Joe. Take that off now!"

"Yes, sir!" Joe turned his back to the audience, struggled momentarily, and then his hands appeared at the bottom of the straitjacket. He lifted it over his head, turned back around to the crowd, and said, "Whew! Glad I'm free of that!"

"Thanks, Principal Johnson. I'll take that diploma now." With one hand holding his diploma and the other carrying the straitjacket, Joe exited the stage to laughter and applause.

"I knew he had something planned," Steve said to Bill. "It figures that it would be with some sort of magic trick."

"It is good they let him graduate. It doesn't look like they can do anything about it now. It was pretty funny, though."

Bill chuckled and took a few more photos before taking his seat.

***

After order was restored and the rest of the graduating class received their diplomas, everyone was invited to meet in the garden area beside the home economics building. It was quite crowded, but finally Bill and Steve were able to find Beth and Joe. They were standing next to a trumpet vine that scaled the building's brick wall. It was in full bloom and was a nice backdrop for photos.

"Nice trick, Joe," Bill said. "You must have been practicing that for a while. I didn't know you had a straitjacket."

"I rented it from a company on the Internet. Good ones are pretty expensive and I didn't want to have to buy it."

"Smart, I suppose," Steve said as he shook his head from side to side and chuckled. "I guess it could have been worse, knowing you."

Then, just as Bill took Beth's diploma to look at it, a hummingbird flew between the two of them and hovered near one of the trumpet vine's flowers. They held completely still as they watched its wings beating frantically as its body was suspended in air. Then it flew between them again and disappeared.

"Oh, Mom. I miss you, too," Beth said quietly. Her eyes, wet with tears, met her father's, and they smiled at each other. Then, hugging each other tightly, they said, "I love you."

"Beth and I are meeting everyone at the river to sign yearbooks and camp out tonight. Can I take some food from the house?" Joe asked.

"Sure, take what you need. Just don't get into trouble!" Steve said with feigned sternness.

"Don't worry. I'll keep him in line!" Beth laughed and grabbed Joe by the arm. There was a twinkle in their eyes that was frequently present when they looked at each other.

"Let me know if there's anything you need," Bill said. "We'll leave and let you kids get to your party."

***

The weather could not have been more perfect for camping. The moon was full enough to see the shimmering water and a slight breeze kept the mosquitoes from buzzing around them. The members of the Totem Club, as well as a few other friends, placed their sleeping bags around the campfire and prepared to write in each other's yearbooks. There was a page dedicated to the Totem Club, as Sammie was able to convince the yearbook staff to put a photo of the group in it.

As they passed around their books, they reminisced about how the club had been started and the places they had met for meetings over the years. Those times were officially over, but they pledged to each other that their friendships would last.

"I have a surprise for everyone," Sammie announced. Everyone became quiet as Sammie, who had grown to be stunningly beautiful, rummaged through a grocery bag that she had hidden in her sleeping bag. She produced a stack of magazines and handed one out to each of them.

"Please turn to page eighty-nine."

They turned to the page and saw a half-page ad with a photo of Sammie looking over a small bridge and throwing flower petals into a stream. Beside her was a bottle of perfume from the company that she had sent her portfolio to a few months earlier.

"How cool!"

"Is that really you?"

"When did you have this taken?"

"Did they pay you for this?"

"You look gorgeous!"

"The magazine will hit the shelves in a few days." Sammie smiled broadly as she explained. "These are copies the perfume company let me have. Remember when I said I was going to visit my grandparents over Easter vacation? Well, I lied. I went to Vegas for a photo shoot. That's where this was taken. I've signed a contract to go to L.A., and I leave the day after tomorrow. I wasn't sure it was going to happen, so I didn't want to tell anyone yet."

"This is so exciting!" Beth walked over to Sammie and gave her a hug. "What did your mother say?"

"Nothing. She doesn't know. I'm going to tell her tomorrow.

She won't want me to leave, but I can't stay here anymore. It's my life now."

Her friends knew how much Sammie had cared for her mother through the years and were not surprised by her announcement. Beth had only been to Sammie's house a few times, but had seen the dirt and clutter. Sammie's room was always tidy and clean, however.

"You guys will be leaving, too," Joe said to Tim and James. They were going to Billings, Montana, to work on a large cattle ranch. The outdoor life of cowboys suited them well and they had learned much about farming by working at their uncle's ranch during the summers.

Tim nodded his head. "Yup, not too long. We've got to help Uncle Sid for a couple of weeks with for first-cut hay. Then we'll be heading out."

"We'll miss you. You'll have to send us a postcard once in a while," Beth said.

"And don't get too saddle sore," added Wyatt.

"Where are you going first, Wyatt?" James asked.

"Munich, Germany. It's where my ancestors were from. The architecture there is something else." Wyatt's voice raised in excitement as he thought about the many places he would study before attending Cambridge University. The United Kingdom was a far cry from Sweet River. Wyatt talked about how had planned on studying firsthand the ancient architecture of the Greeks, Romans, and Egyptians. None of his friends doubted that he would become very successful in his own right. He had received scholarship offers from many colleges and universities in the United States, but he ultimately decided on the place that would get him the furthest from Sweet River.

"You can keep track of me on my blog. I'll be posting pictures, too."

***

As the sky filled with stars, Joe pondered (as he often did) the wonders of black holes, planets, and comets. He and Beth snuggled together on their sleeping bags and made wishes on falling stars as the embers burned low. Quiet snores came from the direction of Tim and James's sleeping bags.

"Are you sorry that you are staying here and not leaving town like our friends are?" Joe asked. "Do you ever feel like I am holding you back from something?"

"No. Never." Beth took Joe's hands within her own. "I know that I want to be with you wherever you are. This has always been my home and—as much as I am sorry to see our friends leave—I still have you. That's the best part of all." Beth's kiss made a small smacking sound.

"Get a room," Wyatt said sleepily. His bag was next to theirs and, being a light sleeper, had heard the entire conversation. Wyatt turned over, put his hands over his ears, and wiggled deeper into his sleeping bag.

"We'd better be quiet," Beth whispered.

"Yeah, well I can be as noisy as I want." Joe raised his voice louder with each word he spoke. "In fact, I want everyone to hear exactly what I have to say. Get up, everyone. I have an announcement to make."

Groggy curses and protests came from the sleepy campers. One by one, they acknowledged Joe's yelling and—when he knew he had everyone's attention—he continued.

"All of you will be leaving Beth and I behind on your grand adventures," he said with a flair and wave of his arms. "So I would like you to share one more thing with us before you depart this pitiful little town."

"Joe, what are you up to?" Beth said.

"Nothing, my dear. But it means everything to me."

Kneeling in front of Beth on the sleeping bag, Joe took Beth by the hand and said, "Beth, will you marry me?"

"Like that is a big surprise!" Tim said sarcastically.

"Shut up, Tim." James nudged his brother.

Beth looked at the big brown eyes that she felt she had known forever. She smiled widely and said, "Of course, I will." This was followed by a long, passionate kiss.

"Yeah! Now can we get back to sleep?" Wyatt said with a yawn.

"Congratulations, you two! I knew it would happen someday. And I know you'll be very happy." Sammie gave them both a hug and said, "You make sure I get an invitation to the wedding or I will never forgive you!"

Joe replied, "Don't worry. You will all be invited and we will make sure you'll have plenty of time to get here. I'm thinking next summer sometime. What do you think, Beth?"

"That sounds like a long time away, but … okay, I guess."

Areanna

Additional angels gathered to assist Joe and Beth's friends on their respective paths. This momentous time required coordination and guidance.

Any time there is a major move, problem or decision facing someone on Earth more angels are present to support the soul, giving them additional strength, protection and direction, if necessary. New people, places, and events have the potential to assist in each individual's soul growth—even if the experiences could be perceived as negative or bad.

It is interesting for us to witness a person who has experienced a challenging situation say, "While I was in the middle of it, I wanted to be done. Now I realize that it was the best thing that could have happened to me. I am who I am because of it. It made me stronger and I would not be where I am today if I had not gone through that terrible time."

Of course, the person had more than likely forgotten what they had previously planned to experience in order for them to grow as a soul. It helps if the person is open and receptive to lessons and choices, realizing that everything they experience is for their benefit and there is potential for them to learn from it.

Even though Joe and Beth would not be leaving Sweet River right then, they had additional stresses and decisions to make as they planned their wedding and their future as a couple. They no longer considered themselves children, but adults.

CHAPTER 10:
JOINED TOGETHER

"I just wish that my mom was here. She would have loved this," Beth said wistfully to her bridesmaids as they were gathered at the Sweet River Reception Center. "Except that she would have insisted on my wedding being at the church. Joe would not agree with having our wedding there, so here we are. It's okay, I guess."

Beth glanced around the room. There were two freestanding mirrors and three sitting tables, along with a bench near the door to the ladies' room. A wicker birdcage hung from the ceiling in the corner m near the window. The curtains were bright yellow with a ruffled valance. The material matched a large bow at the top of the birdcage. There was no bird in the cage, and it was covered with pink, yellow, and orange plastic flowers.

Emma, Jill's only sister, stood next to Beth. Emma did not have her sister's kinky hair, but she had the same bright eyes and engaging smile. Their stature and mannerisms—even the tone in their voices—were also similar.

Beth thought that it was nice to have Emma's presence at the wedding. But try as she might, Emma knew that she was a poor substitute for her younger sister right now. She gently put her arms around Beth and hugged her tightly. "Your mom is here. I am sure of it. She wouldn't have missed this for the world."

"I just hope you are right. It feels like she has been here all along, helping me pick out my dress, the flowers, and the cake. It's just not the same, though." Tears began to trickle down from her hazel-green eyes.

Sammie stepped forward with a tissue and dabbed at Beth's cheeks as she spoke. "Don't mess up your makeup, Beth! We don't have time to do it over."

Drawing in a deep breath, Beth looked at her reflection in the ornate antique mirror.

"Thanks, Sammie. Have I thanked you enough for coming to my wedding? Was it tough to leave the glamorous life of a model and return to this sad little town?"

"Not by a long shot! It is a good break for me. I get so tired of being told what to do, where to stand, and how to turn over and over again. I like the final product, but I get so sick of the long photo shoots. And, I have to admit, the pay isn't bad, either. But the noise and all the people in L.A. get to be too much at times. But this day isn't about me. It's about *you*! Just look at you. You are gorgeous! I know you'd probably feel better in jeans right now, but that dress is beautiful on you."

"Yeah, well, what do you think of my shorts then?" Beth lifted her dress, revealing a pair of worn cutoffs and a lace garter belt on her right thigh. Everyone laughed. "I can't stand thinking that

Joe's going to take this garter belt off my bare leg with everyone watching. This way if he pulls my dress up too far ... voila!"

"With Joe and his magic tricks, it's hard to know just what he'll do," Sammie replied.

The organ music became louder with the familiar strains of "Canon in D." Everyone in the room stopped to listen to the last song before "Here Comes the Bride." Each young lady checked her makeup, grabbed her bouquet, and checked her appearance in the mirrors.

Emma took Beth's face in her soft hands. "You are a lovely bride. I hope you will be very happy. Joe is a wonderful man, and it is nice that you are marrying your best friend. I couldn't be happier for you."

"Thanks, Aunt Emma. I feel pretty lucky myself. Guess you'd better get in your places."

Everyone quickly exited the door among squeals of laughter and excitement.

Bill waited respectfully until everyone but his daughter had left the room. He tentatively peeked through the door and asked, "You ready?"

"Not quite, Dad. Come in." Beth motioned for him to close the door and sit in one of the overstuffed chairs. She pulled a beauty table seat in front of him.

"Thanks for everything, Dad." Beth spoke quickly so as not to give in to the emotions that rose in her chest, attempting to choke her.

"You don't have to thank me." Bill took her hands in his.

"Yes, I do. I know it hasn't been easy raising a girl alone—

and not just any girl. You had to raise me. Ha ha!" Beth smiled sincerely at her father. "You're the best." Bill took in a deep breath and swallowed back the tightness in his throat. He smiled through the tears that threatened to fill his eyes as he looked lovingly at her. She reminded him so much of Jill at times such as this.

The organ music paused and then they heard the first strains of "Here Comes the Bride."

Bill practically leaped out of the chair. "That's our signal, sweetie!" He held out his right arm for Beth. She knew that she would need the support for her shaky knees.

"Okay. Here we go." Beth wrapped both arms around his extended elbow and pulled him down toward her. She quickly gave him a peck on the cheek, wiped off the lipstick, and took a deep breath. Then they both exited the door and down the short hallway to the chapel.

Joe was all smiles as Beth walked toward him. James and Tim, looking fit and tan, were beside him. Their work on the ranch in Montana had matured them physically and mentally. They had confidence, maturity, and strength. Wyatt was obviously absent since all attempts to reach him had been unsuccessful. No one had heard from him in months. His last known address had been in Russia.

The small crowd whispered and nodded their heads approvingly as Beth glided to the pulpit. Most of the neighbors and friends in the wedding party had never seen Beth in a dress or her hair adorned in any way. Beth's hours of practicing walking in high heels at home had paid off—even if her feet were killing her. No one needed to know that she had vowed to lose the shoes at the earliest convenience.

Bill nodded at Joe, kissed Beth on the cheek, and took his seat in the front row next to Emma. Steve was seated on the groom's side next to his older sister, Misty.

Misty lived in Northern California. Joe referred to her as his "old hippie aunt" after she had shared stories of her wild and crazy days in San Francisco during the 1960s. She had long since given up the hallucinatory drugs that were so prevalent during that turbulent time. After experimenting with the least dangerous ones, she realized that they were not for her. During the ensuing decades, she had continued her study of various religions and belief systems. She was known for her lively discussions regarding creation, reincarnation, meditation, God (including all of His various names and where they came from), and any topic in between. Ultimately, she maintained her personal spiritual beliefs, which included a deep love of Mother Earth (and all creatures that inhabited her, including humans) and of God, whom she believed "loves everyone and everything unconditionally, perfectly, and completely."

As odd as it seemed to her only nephew, most people genuinely responded to Misty with kindness. Once a person looked past her odd way of dressing, they could see in her eyes a vision of seeing past the human experience, which she referred to it as "stuff," and acknowledge each person as unique and of value. She also employed a perpetual smile.

Misty was dressed in a tie-dyed scarf-dress of blues, greens, and fuchsia. Her thin salt-and-pepper hair was pulled up simply off her neck and piled in long loops, held together with a variety of colored plastic flower clips. Her handmade, hemp and crystal earrings hung down to her shoulders, matching her necklace, bracelet, and anklet. A faint odor of patchouli surrounded her. Joe briefly looked at his father and jokingly wondered if the excess moisture in Steve's eyes was caused by emotions or the essential oil.

Joe's attention was brought back to the event that he had been planning and thinking about for years. He had known as a young teenager that this woman standing beside him would share his life and he would never let her go. An unmistakable bond held them together and Joe recognized that Beth was his soul mate—even though the term did not always touch what he felt and knew to be certain: Beth was a part of him.

Beth wasn't the type of girl to get emotional or mushy with Joe when he talked about how he felt—even though a surge of chills overtook her at times. Those were the times that she could not deny that there was something very special about their relationship and she knew that she loved him.

Beth took Joe's hand, and they turned to give attention to the weathered face of the priest that Beth had known since she was a child. Pastor Moore's aged hands shakily held a piece of paper in front of him. They were his trusty notes, which his wife had prepared for him earlier in the week, even though he would not need them. His memory was still sharp. He nodded at Beth and Joe. He had watched the couple play at the park, attended many of their school functions, and visited each of their homes throughout their childhood. He officiated at Jill's funeral and helped Bill through his grief. The pastor had officiated at more weddings than he could remember, but he would not forget this wedding any time soon.

"Isn't it wonderful to see best friends grow up to be a loving couple? Today Joe and Beth want to seal that love by the bonds of holy matrimony," he began. "And Beth is in a dress! Can you believe it?"

"Nope," Joe said. With that, the crowd started laughing. Beth's cheeks turned bright red, and she hit Joe with her simple bouquet of daisies and baby blue ribbons. He quickly said, "Sorry. Go on, Pastor."

A sharp breeze blew open a window on the bride's side and the subtle scent of roses wafted from the simple garden below. As Bill and several other men stood up at the same time to close the window, a hummingbird flew in and circled the chapel. Everyone stopped and watched in amazement as it zoomed and soared, seemingly oblivious to the ceremony. It came very close to Beth, who held very still and smiled sweetly. Only Joe could hear her whisper, "I love you, too, Mom," before it took its leave out the same window it had come in.

"That is a first, I must say," said Pastor Moore. After he restored order, he proceeded with his words of wisdom to the couple, his admonishment to those attending the wedding to love one another and support the new couple, and a sincere and heartfelt thanks to his wife of sixty-two years.

Pastor Moore continued, "Now, let us get down to business. Please face each other and hold hands. Joe, do you take Beth to be your beloved partner in life? Will you honor her for who she is and continue your beautiful friendship throughout the rest of your lives here? Will you see in her the soul that she is and help her become what she will be in love and joy?"

Joe nodded, looked deeply into Beth's eyes, and said, "Yes, I will."

Beth took a deep breath. Now it was her turn.

"Now, Beth. Will you take Joe to be your beloved partner in life, to honor him and be his best friend, recognizing the significant soul that he is and allow him to be that every day in love and joy?"

"Yes, I will," Beth said softly.

"Do you have the ring?" Pastor Moore asked Joe. Joe smiled and turned to his best man. Tim patted every pocket in his jacket and pants, but could not feel the ring that Joe had given him that morning. Beth's smile began to fade, and there was a slight murmur of laughter coming from the attendees.

"That's okay, Tim. I think I know where it is," Joe finally said after Tim threw his hands up in the air. His face was bright red, and his brow was moist with sweat.

Joe reached over to Beth, looked behind her right ear and in the flower bouquet. He continued to look behind her as she became more and more annoyed by his antics. Pastor Moore began to chuckle and allowed Joe to have all the time he needed—and seemed to relish—in his search for Beth's missing wedding ring.

"Come on, Joe. That's enough of the magic trick," Beth said sharply under her breath. "It's not funny."

"Oh, wait. I think Pastor Moore has it." Joe reached behind the pastor's right ear and pulled his hand back to reveal the missing ring. A few members of the wedding party chuckled and clapped as Joe bowed slightly to the crowd.

"Whew! You had me a little worried," the pastor remarked in feigned relief. "Now, please place the ring on Beth's finger. This represents the unending love you have for her and will be a reminder to her." Joe placed the ring on Beth's finger and quickly kissed the back of Beth's hand.

"Beth, do you have a ring for Joe?" Pastor Moore asked.

Sammie handed something to Beth. Beth gave her a wink and turned to Joe.

"Please place the ring on Joe's finger. This represents your unending love for Joe and will be a reminder of your love of him every day."

Beth took Joe's hand and placed the ring on his finger, but it didn't feel right to Joe. He didn't get a good look at it because Beth's hand blocked his view. He thought that it felt flexible—like plastic.

Suddenly, Beth moved her hand to reveal a squirt ring pointed right at Joe. Before he had time to react, Beth squirted him right in the face. The bridesmaid line started laughing first. They were in on the joke and had kept it secret from the others. Cameras caught the priceless look on Joe's face. It would not be the last time that Beth was able to pull a joke on Joe.

Through his laughter, Pastor Moore said, "I now pronounce you husband and wife. Please, Joe, kiss your bride!"

Cheers arose in the little chapel as the new couple sealed their love with a kiss. Bill, Emma, and Steve weren't the only ones wiping tears from their eyes.

Areanna

Komsayah smiled as the scene unfolded. She had known about Jill's plan to attend the wedding and, as always, was very supportive.

"Guiding the hummingbird through the window was very nice, don't you think? Thanks for your help," Jill said to Komsayah as they watched the festivities from the garden.

The Lullaby played softly as birds sang and a gentle breeze blew through the lush surroundings. The garden had been designed by Jill and had many of her favorite flowers and trees that she had enjoyed in her various lifetimes on Earth. She enjoyed the warm sun and the many hummingbirds that surrounded the feeders and flowers.

"It was certainly memorable for everyone, I am sure." Komsayah allowed a hummingbird to land on her hand, and she smiled as it acknowledged her and shared the energy of love. The beat of its wings added to the Lullaby, making the experience even more joyful.

There was no sadness or remorse in Jill's voice or demeanor as she watched Beth and Joe exchange vows. "Oh, Beth! Look at you, trying to get one over on Joe with the squirt ring," Jill said, and she started to laugh. "And I thought the hummingbird would be what people might remember. That was for you and Bill, you know," Jill directed to them from a place deep in her soul.

Then, turning her energy completely to Bill, her thoughts were clear and direct. "I am with you," Jill whispered as she looked lovingly at Bill. She reached her hand forward, closed her eyes, and imagined feeling his cheek as she tried to brush a tear away from his cheek.

At that very moment, he reached his hand to his face. It felt as if he had touched something tangible, yet invisible. He sucked in his breath as a wave of love enveloped him. He did not want to cry, but it was impossible not to. Dropping his head for a few moments, Bill thought, *I love you, Jill. I wish you were here.* He clearly heard her say, "I am." His chest—just a few moments earlier had been constricted as he fought to catch his breath—filled with a wave of warmth and peace. He was finally able to inhale deeply as he wiped away his tears and lifted his head. Emma squeezed his hand quickly.

"May we join you?" Sarah asked as they approached Jill and Komsayah. "I hope this is a good time to see the wedding."

"Hi, Sarah. It is always a good time here, isn't it?" Jill chuckled as they embraced. Areanna and Komsayah took each other's hands, and their energy of love increased as a soft glow filled the garden.

"Isn't this fun? I love how you directed the hummingbird through the window. They really respond to you." Sarah observed the multitude of colorful birds as they darted about the beautiful flowers and vines.

"Did you see how Beth and Joe exchanged rings?" Jill asked.

"That was great! I have a feeling they are going to be great parents for me this time. It won't be long and I will be there. I'm getting pretty excited," Sarah answered.

"Just remember as much as you can and I will be around to

keep track of you. Your lessons are important and I will do what I can to help," Jill assured Sarah.

Sarah said, "I know you will. So will the rest of our soul family and all of our guides and angels. It will be a great life for me—I just know it."

Areanna approached the two souls. "Komsayah and I would like to suggest situations, music, and places that could help you to remember each other after you have incarnated, Sarah. Perhaps you and Jill can discuss possibilities before it is time for you to be born."

Jill put her arm around Sarah's shoulder. "Oh, I've been thinking about that." A big smile spread across her face. "They might even surprise Beth and Joe. Let me tell you what I'd like to do."

The two souls shared their ideas and laughed at possibilities and the impact they could have on the souls on Earth. Soon more soul family members, angels, and guides joined them in the garden.

You're the Only One for Me

(Beth)
Was it destiny
The first day that we met?
We were pretty young
That day I'll not forget
All I know is
You're the only one for me

When I've needed you
You've always been there for me
More than my best friend
I think that you'd agree
The only thing I know is that
You're the only one for me

(Chorus)
Don't know why it is
Or what it will be
But I give you my solemn vow
Today I take your hand
Along with my heart and soul
Cause you're the only one for me

(Joe)
I can't think of a day
I wouldn't want you by my side
When we're walking arm in arm
It fills my heart with pride
All I know is

You're the only one for me

I thank the stars above
I think the angels lent a hand
For our lives to fall in place
Like everything was planned
The only thing I know is that
You're the only one for me

(Bridge)
Never will I stray
To you I'll give my love
Today I take your hand
Swear to the heavens above
Along with my heart and soul
'Cause you're the only one for me

CHAPTER 11:
LIVING THE DREAM

"Our truest life is when we are in our dreams awake."
—Fortune Cookie

"I had the craziest dream last night," Beth said sleepily. Joe was struggling to find the button on the alarm clock. Six o'clock was too early to him. "Will I ever get used to this?" Joe asked and moaned as his head hit the pillow for the third time. Steve would be at their apartment in thirty minutes to drive the two of them to work. This was an extra shift for them and the money from the overtime would certainly come in handy.

Joe yawned loudly, smacked his mouth, and noticed how bad the taste was. Not wanting to breathe in her direction, he kept his face turned the opposite way. "What was it about?" As much as he wanted to listen to Beth, he would much rather have gone back to sleep. After all, it was Saturday and he really did not want to go to work.

Their old Totem Club friends were going swimming that afternoon and Joe was more than disappointed about not being able to join them. Beth and Joe had not seen some of their friends since their wedding, so this time was precious to both of them. It would be a time to renew their friendships, catch up on news, and reminisce about old times. Sammie was planning on picking Beth up later and meeting Tim and James at the quarry.

Beth gathered her thoughts about her dream and began speaking. "I was in a garden and there were lots of flowers and trees. It was beautiful. It reminded me of the types of gardens my mom would show me in magazines—with ponds and trails and arches with vines. There were all kinds of birds and butterflies. I remember that there was a hummingbird that kept following me around, and it was leading me down a certain path. If I tried to stop and look at something, it would buzz around my head until I started following it again." Beth stretched and rolled over toward Joe.

"Are you listening to me?" Beth spoke directly into his ear as he lay very still. She was certain that he had fallen asleep until he opened his mouth to answer her.

"Oh, I am listening. I only wish I was asleep. Do you think they'd fire me at the mill if I was late again?"

"Don't even talk like that! You are getting up right now." With a shove from Beth, Joe moved toward the edge of the bed, dropped his feet and legs over the side, and pushed himself slowly to a sitting position. He had several cowlicks, which Beth reached over to smooth. There would be no way to tame them without water.

"Do you think the baby will have your hair?" Beth used her

right hand to rub her rounded abdomen. "It would suck if she had all these cowlicks."

Joe twisted to face Beth. "She will be gorgeous and look just like you," he replied and bent forward to kiss Beth. "She probably will have your crazy, curly hair and then you'll wish she had *my* cowlicks." He laughed and attempted to run his fingers through her hair.

"I wonder if I'll ever get my shape back. Just put a big eyeball on my belly and call me Mike."

"What are you talking about? Mike who?"

"You know, Mike Wazowski from *Monsters, Inc.* Billy Crystal's character. Don't you think I could pull that off with my skinny legs?"

"Sure." Joe laughed.

"Just don't call me that for too long after I deliver—deal?"

"Deal." They shook hands and chuckled.

"So," Joe said as he stood and stretched, "you were saying something about a dream? I've got to get going. Do you want to tell me now or wait until later?"

"Oh, yeah. No, I want to tell you now." She followed him around their small apartment and spoke quickly as he washed his face, smoothed his hair, and made toast.

"I told you about the garden and the hummingbird, right?" Joe nodded as he chewed his toast and drank straight from the milk jug. "It led me to a place where there were nice little garden benches, very ornate. I sat on one and was looking around when my mom showed up beside me." Beth swallowed hard, attempting to hold back the tears and steady her voice as she continued.

"Mom looked great—happy and young. She smiled at me and told me that she is watching as the baby grows. She told me the name we should give her."

Joe stopped what he was doing and looked at her. "I thought we'd already decided on a name. Now we are going to change it again?"

"I really think I had this dream for a reason and she wanted me to know what we should name her. It's Sarah." Beth stopped talking and watched for Joe's reaction. He blinked a few times, and then he turned to look out of the window over the kitchen sink.

"I didn't want to tell you this because I thought it was crazy," he finally replied. "I had a dream last week. There was a cute little girl—about three or four years old—holding my hand and chattering away as we walked toward a park. She kept calling me "Daddy." Beth held her breath as Joe continued, the scene playing out in his head.

"Anyway, she ran ahead of me and started climbing up a tall, slippery slide. I yelled at her and said, 'Sarah Joe Neal. You get down right now.'"

A wave of chills ran up Beth's arms and neck. She rubbed them briskly and started laughing nervously.

"That's it, then. That's her name!" Beth excitedly spoke. "Sarah Jo Neal. I like it. Let's spell her middle name with just a J and an O, okay? It sounds more like a girl name that way."

"Sure, why not." Joe smiled warmly, hugged Beth tightly, and gave her a kiss that was abruptly interrupted by the sound of a horn honking outside.

"There's your dad. I gotta go. I'll call you later. Maybe we can go to the quarry with everybody later? I'll see if I can get off work in time to go."

"Okay, I'll just be here doing laundry and cleaning. Love you. Have a good day at work." She walked with Joe to the door.

"Love you, too. Bye." Joe gave Beth a quick kiss on the cheek and walked to the passenger side of the truck. Steve rolled down his window and leaned out.

"You're looking radiant, Beth. Prettier every day," Steve called.

"Oh, please! I feel huge and I've still got a couple of months to go, but thanks anyway."

"No matter. You're still radiant. Bye now." With a groan from the old truck's gears, Steve and Joe pulled out of the parking lot.

Areanna

"That was fun, I must admit," Sarah said after we watched Joe leave for work. "I wasn't sure Joe had paid attention to the dream. I know he's been open about getting messages from dreams in past lives, but he hadn't been saying much about it in this life."

"No, not too much," I agreed. "There were times when he seemed to consider the possibility of Samantha's dreams having any real meaning when the Totem Club met years ago. Beth definitely got the message loud and clear from Jill this time."

"And I heard *my* name spoken," Jill said as she appeared next to Sarah. "Beth certainly heard *your* name, didn't she," Jill placed an arm around her shoulders. Everyone chuckled and nodded.

"I am having fun visiting my next physical body now and then," Sarah said. "I find it fascinating watching my new body grow. It is a miracle, isn't it?"

Jill said, "There is such a great connection between you and Beth. Even though, in this incarnation, she wanted to be a tomboy, Beth still had her soft side. I remember giving her a doll and hoping that she would play more with it than she did with the trucks and pocketknives that Bill gave her. Once in a while, I would catch her playing with it, but it wasn't very often. And Joe certainly has a soft spot for you in his heart."

"That is true. He has been my father in other lifetimes and I wanted him to play that role for me again this time. He has things he will teach me as we agreed upon in the planning stages here." Sarah smiled as she thought about gathering her soul family together and using a Possibilities Board. "I remember the lessons we thought we could learn and how we would interact with each other, but that can change, considering how much we forget on Earth."

CHAPTER 12: REMINISCING

As the group approached the quarry, they noticed that the familiar path was slightly overgrown with weeds and the surrounding vegetation was becoming brown and dry. It had been an unusually hot summer with very little rain.

"God, I've missed it here," Joe said quietly to himself. "Sure am glad they let me off work early so I could come. They didn't want to pay me overtime for today, so they were happy to let me leave."

"Sammie, have you ever been to the quarry? It sure is nice to see you again," Beth said. "It's like old times having you here with the rest of the club."

Sammie replied, "I have really missed Sweet River, that's for sure. L.A. is nothing like here."

"I don't remember if we'd ever showed you this when you lived here," Tim said as he walked ahead of the group.

"No, I haven't been here. We used to go to the river, but this seemed like the place only the boys would come. It always sounded a little too dangerous for me," Sammie said. "I have to say that it looks familiar somehow." She looked around slowly, squinting at the trees and the bright sun.

"We're almost there," James said and he quickened his step. "It's quite the jump. Are you going to jump today, Sammie?"

"No way, my friend. I really don't like heights that much. I'll just climb down with Beth and watch you guys do the crazy stuff. We'll just be at the bottom to pick up the pieces."

"Don't say that! It freaks me out watching them anyway," Beth said.

The edge of the quarry came abruptly into view and the group slowed to look down. Sammie had a puzzled look on her face. Wyatt noticed it and asked, "What's up, Sammie?"

"I don't know. Maybe I've just seen this in a picture or something, but it looks familiar. Oh, well. Come on, Beth. I'll help you down." Sammie took Beth's arm as they struggled to navigate the rocky trail down the edge of the quarry to the water's edge. The unusual rocks that surrounded them and the echo of their voices added to the Sammie's ominous feeling.

By the time they had reached the shallow water and dropped the picnic lunch on the ground, Beth and Sammie looked up at the group. The young men were gazing down at the water, considering their options for places to jump.

As Joe peeled off his T-shirt, dropped it to the ground, and approached the edge, Sammie suddenly remembered why this place looked so familiar. It was the place that she had seen in the vivid dream many years earlier—the one that she had shared with them. She knew immediately what was going to happen.

"Don't jump! Joe! Stop! Don't jump!" Sammie screamed as

loud as she could. She turned to Beth, grabbed her arm to get her attention, and said, "Beth, you've got to stop him!"

Beth looked with surprise at Sammie and saw the panic and fear on her face. Before Beth could even open her mouth, the two of them turned to see Joe leap from the edge of the cliff, diving toward the water. It was too late to stop him. The others at the top of the cliff heard the gut-wrenching screams from the women below.

Joe knew when he hit the water that he was probably going to be in trouble. He hadn't heard Sammie and Beth on his way down, but for a brief moment in mid-flight, he thought that the angle of his entrance would bring him dangerously close to the bottom. Because the weather had been so warm that summer and there had been so little rainfall, the water was too shallow to dive in safely.

Too late to stop now. Crap, Joe thought with a sense of detachment. He didn't feel any fear, but rather as if he was watching a movie or experiencing a vivid dream.

Joe did not come up to the surface when the group thought that he should. No one dared breathe as they watched the waves ripple across the surface.

Tim said, "It would be just like Joe to hold his breath and stay under. Ha! That's what he's doing." The fleeting smile left his face and he dared not look at the others to see if they shared his sentiment. Somehow, everyone knew that this could not be further from the truth—but no one wanted to believe it.

An ominous stillness filled the air. A crow cawed as it flew overhead. The silence became too much for Beth and a wailing, guttural scream came from her as she slowly collapsed, clutching her swollen belly.

James, Tim, and Wyatt scrambled down the steep sides of the quarry, but Sammie dove in first. Quickly, the young men joined her and the four of them spread out and searched frantically for Joe. As they surfaced to catch their breath over and over again, Beth watched and thought that they looked like the Whack-a-Mole game from the carnival. A part of her did not want to remember what they were looking for.

Finally, Wyatt saw Joe floating a few feet beneath the surface and grabbed his limp arm, pulling him upward. He yelled to the others as he gasped for air. They swam quickly to his side and held onto him as they pulled his body through the water. Upon reaching the shore, they each held a limb, lifted him, and placed his body near Beth. His head was bleeding.

"He must have struck a rock," James said. "This is bad."

Joe's body was limp and pale. Beth shook him, yelling his name over and over in hopes that he would wake up, but no amount of shaking caused any response.

Tim took Joe's right hand to check for a pulse, but he was not sure if he was feeling his own pounding heartbeat in his fingertips.

"I don't think he's breathing," Tim said, then attempted to fill Joe's lungs with air. Sammie grabbed her purse, pulled out her phone, and called 911. After giving the situation and the location to the dispatcher, she rejoined the others and they took turns performing CPR. Each of them had learned it either during scout training or in a PE class, but none of them had done it on a real person.

After an eternity, the faint sound of a siren could be heard in the distance. It took the two EMTs several minutes to gather their equipment at the edge of the quarry and descend the rocky path. Wyatt, James, and Sammie helped them carry the stretcher and bag of supplies.

Everyone but Beth backed away as the EMTs pulled their equipment out and started to assess Joe's condition. They spoke rapidly to each other about what they were seeing and what they would need. They wasted no time in using a mask and oxygen to fill Joe's lungs with air. They said that they "detected a thready pulse" and told the group that chest compressions would not be necessary.

"You guys did a great job with CPR. You may have saved your friend's life," one of the EMTs said.

Joe's color improved slightly after short time. One of the EMTs slipped a breathing tube down Joe's windpipe.

"This tube will help him even more, so if he vomits, it won't go into his lungs."

Beth was crying quietly and was so weak that she required physical support from Sammie and Wyatt. They watched as the EMTs placed Joe on a stretcher, gathered their equipment, and asked for help in getting everything up to the ambulance. The group slowly climbed out of the quarry.

Areanna

Joe felt somewhat disoriented and noticed a sense of floating above his body as he witnessed the scene below with a sense of detachment—even more than he felt as he was falling and knew he was in trouble. Now he heard the Lullaby and remembered what had happened to his body only a moment earlier. He watched his dearest friends struggle with their emotions, especially Beth. He wanted to comfort her, to reach out and hold her. His spiritual arms encircled her, but didn't feel anything tangible.

Joe sensed a bright light, the scent of roses, and the presence of beings around him. He was drawn to the musical tones and sense of love coming from the light. As he approached, he began to gain a stronger sense of what the voices were saying to him. As he moved closer to the angels and guides, he recognized and communicated with them through his thoughts. *Is this it? Am I done?*

"You are not alone. Do not be afraid. We are here to help you," they said. They continued to surround him and his heart was filled with peace.

As Joe became more and more enveloped in light and sound, he clearly saw each of his angels and soul family members, as well as beings he had known on Earth during this incarnation. Even his earthly mother—whose path it was to leave him when he was still a baby—was standing there with her arms opened wide. Immediately, Joe recognized her soul, her earthly lessons, and how she and Steve had agreed upon her choices. Now—no longer mother and son, but soul family members—they embraced.

"It is so good to see you again, Joe. I have missed you so much," Holly's sweet spirit said to Joe.

"Wow. It really doesn't seem like that long ago that I was here. Time doesn't seem to mean much right now," Joe said.

"That's true. It simply comes together—all events and lives. It is now. That's all there is. Here it makes sense, but on Earth, time becomes an illusion that confuses many souls." Holly moved to Joe's side as another being approached.

"Hey, buddy. How have you been?" The familiar melodious timbre came from David. "Quite an exit, I'd say."

"Well, I did say that I wasn't going to stay very long on Earth for this incarnation. I hadn't planned on being part of Sarah's incarnation, but she really wanted me to go and be her father this time. Where is Sarah anyway?" Joe asked.

"Sarah is attending to Beth, along with a few others from here. Sarah wanted to be there at this time and she knew you would be in good hands here. I am sure it would be fine to communicate with her soon," David said. The two souls began moving toward the brightest of the lights, where the Lullaby seemed to be coming from. The sound of chimes seemed to beckon to Joe.

"What have I done, David? Will my decision to leave Earth now be too hard on Beth? I realize that she has her own soul lessons to learn, but could this be too much for her this time around?"

"Joe, are you having second thoughts about returning now?"

"Yes, I guess I am. Beth and I were able to develop a very special relationship on Earth. I know that there is still much I can learn and grow from in this lifetime," Joe admitted. "And being a father to Sarah again could be very rewarding for both of us.

I know the soul lessons Sarah planned for herself and my return now will not change them."

Kamali, who had been following Joe, joined the conversation. "Joe, what do you want to do? You do have the option of returning to Earth."

"It is so beautiful and peaceful here." Joe closed his eyes and experienced the feeling of utter love and joy from his surroundings. "I haven't forgotten how hard life can seem at times, but there can be much love there, too."

"The choice is yours. You need to choose quickly, however," Kamali said.

David placed an arm around Joe's shoulder. "Follow your heart and your soul's stirrings. You will never go wrong if you do. Ask yourself what would be best for you—and know that you are guided by love."

Kamali agreed and added, "That is the way to be guided in every choice on Earth. We are all with you to support you in whatever you decide."

"I don't want to forget that I was here. I want to tell others what I saw and experienced here. Can you help me with that?" Joe asked Kamali.

"That which is for your highest good and the new direction in your life. Your path may be different now. But all is in perfect order."

"Then I want to go back. Please send me back now."

David leaned close and said quietly, "You know, it was getting just a little boring with most of my close family members on Earth now. I've been keeping an eye on things, but … well, maybe I'll just see you around sometime."

"That would certainly surprise Sarah, wouldn't it? I'll be watching for you, then. But let's keep this our little secret and see if Sarah remembers you."

"Now as I am thinking about it, though, I don't really want any difficult lessons. I think I'll just keep it simple and just be content in gardening or something. This could be very interesting," David said slowly as he contemplated the possibilities.

Practicing Zen
(Sung by David)

It isn't just some old religion
It's a deeper faith, a way of life
Helps a soul gain inspiration
Helps in a world of wrong and right

Practice not having expectations
Listen for guidance, seek for truth
Live in the moment with no hesitation
When it comes to seeing the real you

(Chorus)
It's Zen that keeps me going
Practice Zen every day
In Zen there's peace in Being
So I'll just Be
I'll just Be

Living in the Now might not be easy
Giving my ego up for good
Keeping my mind clear just like Buddha
Hoping my intentions are understood

(Chorus)
It's Zen that keeps me going
Practice Zen every day
In Zen there's peace in Being
So I'll just Be
I'll just Be

CHAPTER 13:
NEW LEASE

As Joe was lifted into the ambulance, Tim thought he recognized one of the EMTs.

"Hey, aren't you Phil? Didn't I go to school with you? You were older, but I remember you," Tim said to the EMT who was attaching wires to Joe's chest.

"Yeah, I'm Phil. I'm kinda busy right now, so let's not go down Memory Lane, okay?" Phil turned back to Joe and watched as the monitor screen lit up and a thin line drew across it. An erratic beeping was coming from it.

"What does that mean? He has a heartbeat, right? I heard you say that before. What do you think? Do you think he's going to be okay?" Tim's rapid-fire questions fell onto deaf ears and Phil and the other EMT continued to check other equipment and pick up the radio to call in their report to the dispatcher.

Tim continued to ask questions and shortened the distance between Phil and himself. No one stepped forward to stop him— even though they all had the same questions in their minds. They wanted to know what was happening.

"Look, just follow us to the hospital. I don't have time for this," Phil shot an annoyed look at Tim, and then continued. "A twenty-one-year-old male."

"Joe is twenty. He's twenty," Beth said loud enough for Phil to hear, then whispered to Sammie, "He's only twenty." A sob broke from her throat as she buried her face into Sammie's shoulder. "And we are having a baby." Only Sammie could understand her last words. She held Beth tightly and whispered words of encouragement and solace as the EMT continued his report.

"Twenty-year-old male who dove into shallow water at the quarry. Probably jumped forty feet. Looks like he hit his head on a rock—has a four-centimeter laceration on his forehead. He has been unconscious and his friends performed CPR on him until we got here. He was probably down about twenty minutes. His pupils are dilated and unresponsive. He does have a pulse—in sinus bradycardia of forty-eight. We intubated him and are bagging him with 100 percent oxygen." Phil's back was turned to Joe as the other EMT attended to Joe.

James, who had been quietly leaning on the back door of the ambulance, watched and wondered if what he was seeing was real. He noticed that the monitor started beeping in a more regular rhythm and he would have sworn he saw Joe's right foot move. *Probably just an automatic nerve thing,* James thought.

As Phil's report to the dispatcher continued—with numbers and descriptions that no one in the group understood—James continued to watch Joe's body. *Oh, I don't know, but was that for real? Did I just see Joe's hand move? No, it couldn't have.*

Phil continued, "He is unresponsive and we did suction some fluid from his lungs."

"What do you mean—*unresponsive*? Look!"

Everyone, including Phil, turned to see where James was pointing. Joe was reaching his left hand up to grab the tubing that was connected to the tube in his throat. The EMT closest to Joe grabbed his hand and pushed it down. "I need some help in here," he yelled to Phil.

Phil dropped the microphone as soon as Joe began trying to sit up and to remove the endotracheal tube.

"Oh, my God! Look, Beth! What is going on?" Sammie pushed Beth away from her chest and pointed her face toward the ambulance. There was a sound of confusion and frantic activity as everyone rushed forward to help the EMTs.

Beth rushed forward, but was unable to see what was happening because her friends were blocking her view. She could only assume that it was something more terrible than the accident. Joe must be dead.

"He can't die. He just can't die. I don't want to be here without him." Beth said with a renewed sense of loss. She turned back to Sammie, who was a step behind her.

"You have your baby to think of. Don't give up yet. I'll go see what is going on." Sammie walked quickly to the back of the ambulance and pushed her way through the small crowd. "What is going on?" What she saw caused her to take a step back. Her mouth dropped open in utter surprise and amazement.

Joe was pushing himself up to a sitting position and turning to look at his friends. He began coughing and laughing at the same time. Sammie continued to step backward, and then turned to run toward Beth.

"He's alive! Beth, get up here!"

Beth saw Sammie's huge smile and noticed that her other friends had similar ones.

"What?" Beth was struggling to make sense of Sammie's words.

"How? What? He's alive?' As Beth moved slowly forward, she felt the baby flip over and kick like she had never done before. Beth's hand went instinctively to her belly and she rubbed it. Her friends parted as she got nearer to the ambulance and her heart beat frantically. She knew that she wouldn't believe it unless she saw it for herself.

"Hi, baby," Joe said as he continued to cough. "Did I scare you? Sure scared me!" Joe's smiling face was the only thing that Beth could see and focus on. Her friends helped her into the ambulance and she sat next to Joe.

Beth was unable to speak, her throat tight and constricted. Joe gently wiped her eyes away.

"Well, I've never seen anything like it," Phil said. "I'd better call dispatch back." He reached for the microphone and shared a look of disbelief with his fellow EMT.

Phil returned to the embracing couple and said, "The hospital wants you brought in for observation. You'll need antibiotics to keep from getting pneumonia from the water in your lungs. Other stuff might happen, too. You really need to be monitored. Plus, you need that head wound stitched up."

"Sure, I guess so," Joe said. Beth nodded her head in agreement.

***

"Can I talk to you about something?" Joe said slowly to the night shift nurse who had walked into his hospital room to bring him a pain pill. The heart monitor beside the bed beeped loudly. Joe had not been able to sleep at all. His head was throbbing and he kept replaying everything that had happened.

"Sure, what's up, Miracle Man?" The veteran nurse was efficiently checking Joe's vital signs, the equipment, and her watch. *Tonight has been lasting forever,* she thought.

"What do you think happens when somebody dies?" Joe slowly sat up and reached for his water glass.

"It is probably more important to ask yourself what *you* think. Look what happened to you today. You could have easily died, but you didn't." She spoke with genuine caring and concern. Her voice felt soothing to Joe.

"Yeah, I could have, I guess. There was something telling me not to jump, but I thought I was just being silly. I used to be really scared to jump—even a little ways—into the water. I worked hard to overcome that fear and now I can jump from quite a height," Joe said proudly.

"I'm sure you can." The nurse pulled a chair close to the hospital bed.

"I knew things were different today. I figured that the water was deep enough and I was with my old friends who I used to go swimming with. It was like old times. I would never have done

129

it by myself, especially since we are having a baby soon." A smile slowly appeared, but disappeared quickly. "I could have made Beth a widow—left her to raise our baby by herself."

"Oh, yeah! I thought I knew who you were. Your wife's mother used to work here, didn't she? Jill Green. I had only been here a few months when she died. That was sad." "Yeah, we were just kids then. Not having a mother around has been hard on her. That's one of the reasons I wanted to know what you thought about what happens when you die. Do you think we go somewhere?"

"I've seen a lot of stuff happen with people when they die. Sometimes you don't think they have a chance and then they surprise you by getting better. Or the young ones die from something simple—some freak accident. And look at what happened to you today. You really were dead!" The nurse leaned closer to Joe and touched his hand. "What happened when you were dead? Do you remember anything?"

Joe could tell from her touch and voice that she sincerely wanted to know. He took a deep breath, looked up at the ceiling, and wondered what he thought he could verbalize. His emotions were close to the surface and he did not want to cry.

"I saw everything happen. What I mean is—it was like I floated up and watched everything. I saw my friends doing CPR and Beth crying. That tore me up because I wanted to tell her that I was okay—that everything was going to be okay." Joe looked intently at the nurse. "It seemed so real."

"Oh, I think it was real. Then what do you remember?"

"Then it seemed to get more hazy, more bright, but ... I don't know. It seemed very peaceful and it was like there was somebody there. Maybe there was even more than one. I remember a song or something like music playing—real peaceful, beautiful."

A buzzer sounded outside Joe's room. The nurse stood up and leaned forward.

"Joe, keep trying to remember. I would love to talk to you more about this, but I have to go help someone right now. I'll be back when I can, okay?"

With a slight slur to his voice, Joe said, "Yeah. I'm really tired right now. I think I'll go to sleep. Maybe that medicine is working because my head doesn't hurt as bad."

"That's good. Get some rest. I'll check on you soon."

Areanna

"Isn't it interesting how some people are open to the possibility that life goes on and there is more to life than what their soul is experiencing on Earth?" I said as we watched Joe peacefully sleeping.

"I wonder how much Joe will remember over time," David said. Po, his angel, leaned over to get a better look at Joe's face.

"He seems glad to be back. What do you think, Kamali?" Po asked.

"He may have moments of clarity. Sometimes this causes the soul to long for home. I know that Joe did not want to necessarily stay long in this lifetime, but choosing to return was an option he had now. That decision may make a difference in the lives of those around him, certainly, but their ultimate lessons will remain the same as they chose before going to Earth," Kamali replied.

We watched Joe, blessing him and his life, filling the spaces and time with love and peace.

"It seems that there continues to be a great controversy in humanity regarding the truth about life-after-death experiences," I said. "The nurse was open to the possibility, but I am sure there will be those that Joe may want to share his experience with that will not believe that it was real. Many scientists believe that the memories of home are simply tricks of a dying brain or the effect of medications. There are other explanations as well, but many individuals—including children—tell of their brief visits here. They may have been experiencing a near-death experience, having a vivid dream, or they simply never completely forgot when they were incarnated.

"For those who have forgotten completely," David said, "all of this can seem very surreal or absolutely crazy. I remember the lifetimes that I did not remember my angels or my soul family. I plan on taking more memories with me this time and staying open to influences, déjà vu, and other things."

"Yes, David," Po said. "I will be there always to assist you to remember and to guide you. It is helpful knowing that the body is simply a vessel—a tool for the spirit to use. The soul is eternal, but the body is not."

CHAPTER 14:
LANDING

Areanna

Loved ones gather for this very special occasion, to bid bon voyage to a soul who is about to be incarnated on Earth. Many individuals will be able to join the soul in various capacities; however, most of them will forget the special connection they shared here. All is in perfect order, of course. There is no sadness in parting, but a sense of hope for soul growth and a joyous return.

We have been together for this type of event countless times. There is our sweet Sarah, other special escorts and guides, numerous soul family members, and me. Some soul family members are already on Earth and are waiting for Sarah to arrive.

Beth and Joe have been progressing on their path toward parenthood. Sarah has visited them and has been checking on the body her soul would soon occupy. This physical form will assist her to do the things that she has planned for her earthly life, so it needed to be healthy and strong.

Sarah will bring to Earth love, hope, inspiration, and other gifts of the spirit. She may be able to tap into memories of home, other incarnations, and soul family members. She and I have determined triggers for this to happen—little reminders that may cause her to have flashes of memories or déjà vu. If she is able to quiet her mind and pay attention, she may even hear the Lullaby and remember her connectedness to all there is.

The atmosphere in Sarah's favorite garden was almost electric with anticipation. Sarah had been flitting around like a little bird, sharing hugs and smiles with everyone. Their inward lights were shining brightly and, like overlapping waves, were intermixing with each other.

"Sarah, it is almost time," I reminded her. "Beth has been in labor and the time is near for you to arrive. It is October 11 on Earth—the day of your delivery."

Sarah made brief final remarks of love to everyone and then returned to my side.

"Okay, I am ready now."

I made our final announcement. "Sarah and I will be leaving now. Our love is with you all."

Suddenly, a brilliant golden light surrounded us. It spread and encircled everyone. Angelic choirs sang of love and peace in perfect harmony, using the Lullaby as their theme.

Sarah and I did not speak, but communicated through thoughts. We shared the experience of traveling to Earth as the beautiful planet got closer and closer.

"Isn't it something? I just think it is a wonderful place. I hope I remember what a blessing it is to visit here," Sarah said as we approached North America. "We are almost there. I am always with you. Please watch for the signs we decided on that will help you remember and be influenced by guides, your other spirit, and me. You will be fine—no matter what. I love you so, you know."

"Yes, and I love you. Stay very close so I can always feel your presence."

Soon we were aware of a shift in the energy field around us after a trip through a tunnel and a dark screen-like material (sometimes referred to as the Veil). The light around us faded and objects became dull and lifeless. The colors were muted and limited in number—nothing like the brilliant variety and depth of hues of home.

Special attending angels were gathered and waiting for us in the delivery room. Mesha and Kamali were next to Beth and Joe. They greeted us warmly and gave us information on Beth's progress as Sarah anxiously watched and whispered to Beth. "I'm here, Momma. Ha, ha. That sounds so nice to call you that. I love you so much."

"Push, Beth. She's almost here. Don't stop pushing. Give it all you can," the doctor said.

Joe suddenly noticed that his knees were weak as he stood next to Beth's head. He thought he heard the word "momma" whispered and wondered whether that was what Sarah would call her. His body began trembling, and he tried to keep his voice from sounding so fearful.

"Come on, Beth. You can do this. I know you can," Joe whispered.

Beth felt very tired after hours of labor. She could not focus her eyes or her thoughts, and she felt a sense of disconnection to everyone and everything around her. She knew that people were speaking to her, but all she wanted to do was sleep.

"Her blood pressure is dropping," the nurse reported.

The doctor took a brief look at the fetal heart monitor, which was sounding out each heartbeat. It was rapid and regular. "Looks like the baby is okay. Just speed up the IV."

Joe felt a sense of panic rising in his chest, and he grabbed the nurse by the arm. "Is everything okay?"

"Everything will be fine. She just needs to get that baby here, that's all. I'm going to get you a chair. You look pretty pale."

Beth was aware of the faint sound of music, like a familiar lullaby. It seemed very strange to her, yet reassuring. She felt as if she were floating up off of the delivery table.

Something made her arm feel very cold and it was annoying to her. *Just let me rest. I just want to rest. Can't they just let me rest?* Beth was becoming more aware of movement and sounds. She started to notice the cramping pain rolling over her abdomen. Her eyes flew open and she looked around the room.

Is that Grandma in the corner? That doesn't make any sense. She is smiling and waving at me. It must be the drugs. Beth took a deep breath and tried to stop herself from screaming as the pain enveloped her.

"Come on, Beth. Push with it," the nurse said.

Beth gripped the handles and started pulling. She thought she saw a wispy, ghostlike figure of a beautiful young woman with long brown hair walking past her. The woman seemed to briefly look around the room, as if she were talking to a crowd, and then disappeared near Beth's feet. Beth blinked her eyes several times in disbelief.

"This is it, Beth. The baby's head is coming. Push!" the doctor yelled.

Beth shook her head, tried to clear her thoughts, and concentrated on what she needed to do. She pulled on the handles, leaned forward, and pushed with all of her might.

"Here she comes. Look, Beth! It's Sarah!" Joe caressed Beth's arm and wiped his tears away to get a better look at his daughter.

The baby's cries filled the room.

***

"Isn't she just the cutest thing ever, Joe?" Beth said as she held Sarah in her arms a few hours later. "Her hair is just the best! Dark brown—like yours. I can't believe how much she has."

"And she's beautiful—just like you." Joe leaned forward and gave Beth a gentle kiss. "You are going to be such an amazing mother."

"I hope so. There is so much I want to tell her, to share with her. We'll take her camping and hiking and—"

"Hold on! You're not going to make her carry her own sleeping bag yet! Let's just let her be a baby for a while. She doesn't need to be fighting off bears until she is a little older, okay?"

"Sure, sure. I won't get her a pocketknife just yet," Beth said as she gave Joe a wink and a smile.

Listen to Your Momma

My baby girl, small for a while
I see your face and smile
My baby girl, my love grows so
There's many things you need to know

I want to teach you about
Living in this crazy world
Finding your voice, making your way
Even though you're "just a girl"

(Chorus)
Just listen to your momma
Don't forget to listen
Listen to your momma
'Cause I've been here, too

I hope you always keep your heart open
I'll always try to raise you right
Teach you to climb the toughest mountains
And then I'll teach you how to fly

You get to choose what brings you joy
Beat the monsters in your dreams
Being wise when your problems arise
Knowing that life isn't all it seems

(Chorus)
Just listen to your momma
Don't forget to listen

Listen to your momma
'Cause I've been here, too

Listen to your momma
Hear what I'm saying, my girl
Listen to your momma
'Cause I've been here, too

My baby girl, small for a while
My love is always with you

CHAPTER 15:
DADDY'S LITTLE GIRL

"Good morning, Sarah. Aren't you looking pretty today in your new outfit? It's your very first Christmas—and it will be so fun."

Joe lifted Sarah from her crib. It was an old wooden one that Beth had slept in as a baby. They had painted it bright yellow to match the walls in the tiny room next to their bedroom. The room was originally meant to be a walk-in closet, but after many tenants and remodels, the shelves and rods had been removed and a small window had been cut through the wall.

Beth painted one wall to look like tiger stripes and had collected as many stuffed jungle animals as she could from the local thrift store. They had put them in a pile in the corner of the room, with a few in the crib and on a small bookshelf. Sarah had received a mobile with giraffes, lions and tigers, which now rattled as Joe gathered a blanket and his daughter to his chest.

Joe had forgotten how many times he had been a mother and a father in other lives—and how well he cared for children—so he handled her more delicately than he really needed to out of fear of hurting her or doing something wrong. As he was relearning his parenting lessons, Kamali watched over him with amusement.

Sarah, trying to focus on Joe's face, slightly curled her bottom lip—and Joe let out a whoop. "Beth, come and look! Sarah is smiling!"

Beth ran into the nursery. "What? Is everything okay? What's wrong?"

"Nothing. I'm sorry if I frightened you. Sarah just smiled!"

"Well, of course she did." Beth looked down at Sarah. "You sweet thing, you."

Sarah let out a little startled cry at the commotion.

"Oh, Joe. I forgot to tell you that a package came yesterday from your Great-Aunt Misty."

"Any idea what it might be?"

"No, but it is heavy and sounds like rocks when I shake it."

"That's probably exactly what it is. You know how Misty loves crystals. Come on, Sarah. Let's go find out. It's time to start opening the presents."

Areanna and Mesha followed along—unseen by everyone but Sarah.

"I'm glad that the crystals arrived. Now Sarah can start benefiting from them," Areanna said.

"Yes," replied Mesha, "and Joe and Beth, too."

***

"Beth, you shouldn't have!" Joe exclaimed. "This is too much." Joe tore back the bright red wrapping paper to reveal a box. The long sticker was a photo of a telescope.

"Well, I know how much you have been wanting one. Now you and Sarah can see the stars even closer."

Sarah was asleep on Joe's chest. Hearing his heartbeat lulled her to sleep after being fed and changed. Joe seemed to be getting better and better at those tasks. Beth appreciated how attentive Joe was as a father. *He is actually a very cute father,* Beth thought. *Look how peaceful Sarah is.*

"Well, if she was awake now, I'd bundle her up and we'd try it out! Thanks so much." Joe leaned over carefully, so as not to awaken Sarah and gave Beth a tender kiss.

"You are so welcome. Let's say that the telescope came from Sarah as well, okay? I'm sure she would agree."

They heard a loud knock on their door. They were expecting their fathers to share Christmas with them. The sound startled Sarah and she started moving about on Joe's chest. Beth jumped up from the floor at the base of their small Christmas tree to answer the door.

Steve's booming voice echoed through their small apartment. Joe did his best to cover Sarah's ears, but it was too late.

"Ho ho ho. Merry Christmas, everyone! And how is my second-favorite girl?" Steve asked Beth as he entered and pecked her on the cheek.

"It is always good to know where I stand, Grandpa Steve," Beth said.

"Oh, I love that title, but it makes me feel just a little old."

By then, Sarah was crying loudly. Joe got up from the floor and walked toward the door.

"Thanks, Dad. How about being a little quieter when you come in? And you could try just knocking gently, okay?"

"Sorry, son. May I hold my favorite girl?" Steve reached out and gently took Sarah in his big, burly hands. She looked especially small and fragile on his chest. He held her like a professional, patted her back, and whispered gently in her ear. Soon she calmed down and stopped crying.

"See, I haven't lost my touch! You were a pretty good baby yourself, Joe. Now let's take a look at that tree, shall we, Sarah?"

A quiet tapping sound came from the door and Beth opened it to see Bill standing there. His arms were filled with brightly wrapped presents. The large bows were lopsided and the tape on the packages was coming loose. Some of the boxes peeked through the wrapping paper and others had two different patterns of paper on them.

"Hi, Dad." Beth gave her father a quick kiss as she took a few of the gifts from his arms.

"Hi, sweetheart. Am I late?" Bill asked.

"No, Steve just got here. I see that you wrapped the gifts yourself. Nice touch."

"Yeah, it's not the same as your mother would have done." Bill's eyes were beginning to shine brightly.

Beth led her father to the tree and they carefully placed the gifts beneath it.

***

The day went smoothly; Sarah was the center of attraction. Even when she was asleep, it seemed that her family couldn't get enough of her.

"Hey, what is this box? I don't remember seeing this," Steve said as he lifted the heavy box of crystals.

"Aunt Misty sent them," Beth said. "There's some beautiful rocks in there."

"Yeah, she loves that kind of stuff. Always has," Steve explained. After a long pause and a deep breath, he continued. "I got a call from her yesterday. Seems like she isn't doing very good. I wanted to talk to you about that." Steve gave Joe a serious look and went on.

"I am not one to mince words, so I won't. Her health is getting poor, and she asked me if you and Beth would move to Glenport to help take care of her."

Silence filled every space in the room and shock registered on the faces of Beth and Joe.

"She wants us to *what*?" Joe turned to Beth for moral support. "That is ridiculous! Why would we want to do that?"

"Just listen for just a minute, son. Please, Beth. Sit down. You don't look so good." Steve took Beth by the arm and led her to an old overstuffed chair.

"Okay, I'll listen, but you'll have to make this good because it will be your only chance," Joe said.

"Misty called me a few weeks ago and gave me a heads up that she was having some tests run because she hadn't been feeling good for a while. Well, the tests came back that she has leukemia. The doctors wanted to start treatments, but she told them that she's lived long enough and just wants to go out naturally."

"And?"

"She's always had money, but you would never know it. She got involved in a mining company a long time ago and it made her a bundle. She didn't want to live large, so she put her money away and just let it grow. Now she wants to share her wealth, but doesn't think it is okay just to give it away. She'd like to give you and Beth a chance to earn it from her by taking care of her until she dies. You can live in the little house on her property—the one behind her house."

"I remember that place. I loved to hide out there when we'd go to visit her," said Joe.

"Yeah. It needs a little work, but she is willing to pay someone to do that if you decide to come."

"But what about work? What could Joe or I do there?"

Steve smiled knowingly and said, "Here's the best part. She wants to pay for school for the both of you. She will help you through college. There's even a community college there that offers classes from the university. Neither one of you will have to work. She said she'd take care of everything."

"Oh, my God," Joe exclaimed. He found the floor the safest thing to sit on, next to Beth. He looked up at her. Both of their faces were pale.

Beth got up from her chair, started quietly crying, and walked silently toward her father. He opened his arms and held her tightly. Neither one of them could speak. After several minutes, Bill broke the silence.

"I already knew about this. Steve and I've talked about it several times. Neither one of us could give you and Joe that kind of chance for a future. And Sarah will be set. Misty has already put her in her will."

With a croaking voice, Beth said, "But I can't leave you here, Dad. I can't leave you alone."

"Yes, you can, honey. Yes, you can. I want you to have a life and this will be the opportunity of a lifetime. Don't worry about me. I will be fine. I'll just have to take more vacations and visit you—that's all."

"Is it settled then? Joe, you're not saying much," Steve said.

"Wow. It is a lot to take in right now. And Misty is kinda weird," Joe said with a smile. Everyone laughed.

"How about letting Beth and I talk about this. How soon would we have to give Misty an answer?"

"She would like you to come as soon as you could. It would be nice if you could give two weeks' notice at the mill. Then Bill and I can take some time off to help you get there."

Beth took another deep breath and said, "How about we let this topic go for the rest of the day. I think we should get dinner going. Is that okay?"

Everyone agreed.

***

The family sat down to Beth's simple, delicious dinner. Her cooking skills had improved over the years, and she definitely had a way with spices. Even though she grew up very much a tomboy, she loved to cook. When Jill was alive, she and Beth had spent many hours in the kitchen concocting wonderful dishes. Even while preparing this dinner, she felt that her mother was near.

By the time dinner was over and the dishes were washed and put away, Steve and Bill gathered their gifts and prepared to leave. It had been an emotional day and everyone was feeling tired. As Beth and Joe walked their fathers to their trucks, everyone suddenly got quiet. None of them said good-bye when they parted; they simply gave each other hugs and kisses. Beth and Joe waved silently at the departing vehicles.

Joe looked up at the sky as he and Beth walked arm in arm to their door. It was early evening and the night sky was covered in stars.

"Well, I think I'll bring that little girl of ours outside to see this," Joe said, and he wrapped Sarah in a blanket.

Beth helped by putting a knit cap over Sarah's head. "I'll let you two enjoy it together. I think I'll go Google Glenport, California. I should know a little more about it before we talk. Enjoy your time with Daddy, Sarah."

Areanna

"When you were very young, were you as fascinated with the night sky as Joe has been?" I asked Carl Sagan.

"Yes. I couldn't seem to get enough of it. I loved the magic and mystery of it all. The constellations captured my attention, but it was absolute endlessness of space that seemed to pull me in. It's nice to see other souls as interested." Carl looked up and smiled as we joined Joe for his first look through the new telescope. "I'd like to see Joe stick with his study of this, now that he has the financial opportunity to do so."

"We shall see. I am sure you will stick around to find out, won't you?" Kamali asked.

"Indeed, I will," Carl said emphatically. "I know that he will have other options to consider, but I am prejudiced, I guess."

"Free will is so necessary in order for the soul to grow in its way, in its own time. I love the perfection of that process," I said. "Beth and Joe, having been given an opportunity by Misty to explore the world more, become educated, and stretch beyond their comfort zones is perfect. But they will ultimately decide whether they will go down that path, having forgotten that this may have been part of the plan from the beginning. We are there to guide, but cannot make those choices for them."

"Of course," Carl said. "But you can't blame a guy for trying."

A Daddy's Love

I may not always be around
To show you the stars in the sky
I may not always get to hug you
Or calm your fears when you cry

But every time you look above
At the stars in the night sky
You'll be reminded that I love you
And here's the reason why

(Chorus)
A daddy's love is like the stars
Always shining through
Just like my love for you

Use the stars to make a picture
Connect the dots to make a bear
Seeing stars with you beside me
I feel like a millionaire

The stars are there when you can't see them
Behind the clouds, behind the moon
If you could add them all together
Wouldn't be as much as I love you

(Chorus)
A daddy's love is like the stars
Always shining through
Just like my love for you

If I could take you for a ride
We'd soar through the night
Float upon the Milky Way
Take Pegasus for a ride

Use a Dipper to get a drink
Ask Orion what he's hunting for
Catch the brightest falling star
There's so much to explore

CHAPTER 16:
IS GOD EVERYWHERE?

Beth sat across a large wooden table from Pastor Moore. The pastor's office was quiet and simply furnished, located at the back of the church behind an ornate door with a large gold knob. Beth's eyes kept looking up at a large painting of Jesus above the pastor's head. The artist's depiction showed a longhaired man with a kind smile and a look of compassion. No matter how many times Beth had been in this office, the painting never seemed to calm her. She felt that the Jesus in the painting was able to see her sins and she would be punished right there on the spot. Beth distracted herself by checking on Sarah, who was asleep on the floor in her carrier.

"Pastor Moore, I just don't know what to do. Joe and I agreed that this move would be a great opportunity for us, but I am afraid that he's going to quit going to church all together. Steve never made Joe go to church much while growing up. Every time I try to talk to him about going to church here or the churches that are in Glenport, he shuts me off. He tells me that he doesn't need to sing songs in a church to feel close to God."

Pastor Moore listened intently, and then he asked, "Why do you think that is?"

Beth adjusted Sarah's pacifier and took a deep breath. "I don't know. I don't think Steve ever belonged to one. At least he never talks about it. They did the usual celebrating religious holidays—the Christian ones anyway. I couldn't talk Joe into getting married in the church, remember?"

"Yes, I remember your wedding. How could I forget? Joe pulled the ring out from behind my ear, and then you used a squirt ring on him. Oh, yes. And there was a hummingbird that came in the window. Quiet memorable." Pastor Moore leaned forward. "Why do you think it is important for Joe to belong to a church now?"

"Well, I want Sarah to have some direction—some guidance—that a church can give her. If Joe and I don't see eye to eye about religion, then what will Sarah believe in?"

"Don't you think Joe believes in God?"

"Yeah, I guess so. He thinks the world is a wonderful place that God created. Is that what you mean? He seems to think that's as far as he needs to believe."

"Religion is more than belief in creation. Doesn't he believe in heaven and hell and life after death?"

"I think so. He almost died a few months ago when he hit his head diving into the quarry. He says that he thinks he went somewhere—like a near-death thing. He doesn't talk too much about it. Maybe it's because I won't listen."

"Well, don't be hard on yourself. You feel strongly about his soul—and for Sarah's. You are trying hard to be a good mom and to bring Sarah up right. But even Jesus did not force people to follow him. He led by example."

"Yeah, you're right," Beth said quietly.

"Here's what I want you to do for Joe. I want you to love him. That's all."

"You make it sound easy."

"You love him now, don't you?" Pastor Moore asked. Beth nodded. "Well, then just keep doing it and Sarah will see that you love him, too. Let God sort out the details later. Let God be the judge of Joe's life."

"Okay, I'll try. But I'm going to keep going to church and taking Sarah."

"Do what your soul directs and listen to your heart. God is always where love is, Beth."

***

She felt a little better after leaving Pastor Moore's office, but Beth still had some nagging questions about what had happened to Joe during his accident. She had not wanted to believe Joe when he tried to talk to her about what happened to him after he "died." It reminded her of how close she had come to being a widow and raising Sarah alone. Now that she had talked to Pastor Moore, Beth felt stronger emotionally and thought that it might be the right time to ask Joe more about that day at the quarry.

When Sarah was asleep in her crib and Joe and Beth were waiting for sleep to come to them, Beth's mind started racing. She tossed and turned and her movements did not go unnoticed by Joe.

"Can't you sleep? You are flopping more than a fish."

"Sorry. No, I can't. Guess I've got a lot on my mind."

"Like the move? That has kept me awake lately." Joe sat up in bed and leaned his head back on the headboard. "Go ahead. Let's talk about it."

"It really isn't the move so much right now, although that does worry me. It's something I've been wanting to ask you about."

"Like what?" Joe asked, becoming a little suspicious.

"It's about what happened during your accident."

Joe rolled his eyes. "Are you going to give me grief again? I told you what I remembered, and you think I was dreaming or hallucinating or something. Why do you want to talk about it now?"

Beth tried hard not to be hurt by his remarks and practiced what she was asked to do today: love.

"Okay. Will you tell me again what you remember? I promise I will listen this time. Please?"

Joe took Beth by the hand and looked directly into her eyes. "This is very special to me, so I hope you will keep your promise."

"I will."

His eyes drifted up and to his right, as if the words and explanations were written on the ceiling. "You remember me telling you about floating up out of my body and I watched the guys doing CPR on me? I felt pretty disconnected to what was happening, so it seemed like a dream. But I knew that it wasn't.

"I remember hearing something like music or singing or a funny beautiful language coming to me from a place away from me, like down the road or something. I felt like I wanted to find out more about it and, as soon as I thought that, there was a really bright light around me."

Sarah shifted her body in the crib and let out a little cry. After a moment of listening, Joe and Beth looked at each other and shrugged their shoulders. Joe continued.

"I remember feeling that there were people around me, but I can't remember who they were. I know that I knew them, though. Like old friends or family. I think one was my mother."

"What? Really?"

"Yeah. My dad doesn't know any of this, so I hope you won't say anything."

"No, I won't. How was that—seeing her?"

"I'm a little fuzzy on that—knowing if it really was her—but I know it felt really good. Like all was forgiven. Like life and what happened here didn't matter. And I know now that she loved me." Joe's voice cracked, and he rubbed his eyes quickly.

Beth put her arms around him and held him tightly as she thought about what must Joe must be feeling. He never talked about his mother and did not know anything about what had happened to her—let alone her reasons for abandoning him. She recalled how she felt when her mother had died and how much she missed her. Joe didn't have any childhood memories of his mother.

"I remember talking to someone about coming back—back to my body. I wasn't sure I wanted to, but I thought about you and Sarah. It felt like I wouldn't be judged either way—like there wasn't a right or wrong choice to make. But then I knew how much I loved you and I didn't want to be without you, so I told them to send me back." Joe took Beth by her hands and looked deeply into her eyes.

"You and Sarah mean everything to me. I hope this move will be good for us. It just seems like the right thing to do. It feels like going home—even though I've been gone from there for a long time."

"We'll be fine. We have each other. I haven't needed another best friend since I cut your butt in that tree," she said with a laugh.

"And I still have the scar to prove it!"

"Thanks for talking to me about this. I'm sorry I didn't listen very good before."

"No worries. Maybe we'd better try to get some sleep before Sarah wakes up."

Areanna

"Joe's experience here during several of his incarnations left with him some important memories. I believe that these memories will give him strength and focus in his life this time to work on the lessons he has yet to accomplish," Kamali said.

"Beth may begin to remember her lessons as well," Mesha added. "She seems to have forgotten what she knows on a soul level regarding religion and spirituality. It seems that for the younger souls, this lesson is a very important one—one that causes a type of blindness to truth."

I nodded my head in agreement. "We are perfect in our

knowledge and have not had to go through the lessons that these souls have had to go through. It is easy and joyful for us to observe their incarnations, but it is out of our understanding to know what it is like to forget and struggle."

"And we know the agreements these souls have made. We will see if their choices and other influences will bring their memories back to them this time," Kamali said. "A deep and abiding love has brought Joe, Beth, and Sarah to this place in their human lives. That is the most important lesson of all."

I gently stroked Sarah's head as she slept. As I hummed the Lullaby, Kamali and Mesha joined me in the beautiful strains and everyone felt an overwhelming sense of peace and love in the home.

When I'm Outside

In my younger days I went to church
Sat and listened to every word
Tried to fit in, it just didn't work for me
Now I found my religion outside where I'm free

What I believe ain't in the pages of your book
Finding my truth came with a second look
I'm not perfect, but God loves me anyway
I'm a work in progress; I'll get to my heaven someday

(Chorus)
When I'm outside God calls to me
I see his holiness all around me
When I'm outside God calls to me
I see his holiness right there in front of me

You don't need to knock on my door
Give me a flyer or bless me anymore
I feel blessed when I step outside
That's where my soul feels all right

From the Next Book in the *Preflight* Series

Joe could see through the large window as he walked up the sidewalk to their front door. Beth was pacing back and forth, turned to see Joe, and practically pounced on him as he opened the door.

"I didn't want to call you while you were in class, but I'm going kinda crazy here." Beth's voice sounded frantic.

"Calm down. Take a breath. Slow down and tell me what's wrong." Joe was alarmed, but knew that he should not add his fear to the moment.

"Have you seen Aunt Misty? When was the last time you saw her? Did she tell you she was going anywhere today?"

"Whoa! Did I say to slow down?" Joe took Beth by her upper arms and led her to one of the old wooden kitchen chairs. "Now, I need you to take a breath before you say anything."

Beth did as she was told, closed her eyes, and inhaled deeply. She opened her eyes slowly, looked directly at Joe, and began speaking calmly.

"I can't find Aunt Misty. She told me this morning that she

was going out for a walk in the woods. I heard on the radio this afternoon that there's a big storm coming."

Joe had noticed during class that the sky had become increasingly darker and the wind had definitely picked up. Even though he was older, he had not stopped daydreaming during class.

"Misty knows what the storms are like here. She watches all the signs and knows them better than we do. Maybe she just went to visit a neighbor or something."

His explanation did not ease Beth's apprehension. "There is something wrong, I just feel it. Joe, this is serious."

Joe had come to respect Beth's intuition. She continued, "The winters here are crazy. I just hate the wind. What if she doesn't get back in time? Should we call the police to start looking for her? Should I ask the neighbors to help?"

Sarah, hearing her parents in the kitchen, left her pile of toys and walked tentatively to her father's side. She reached her little arms up and he gently picked her up.

"Hi, sweetheart? How are you?" Joe kissed her on the cheek and gave her a squeeze. Her little arms wrapped around his neck.

"Joe, please. We've got to talk about this. We have to figure out what to do," Beth pleaded.

"Okay. Let's call the neighbors and see if anyone has seen her. That will be a good start."

Conclusion

There appear to be many more questions than answers in life's journey. As you look around, you may see what others believe to be the solutions to every existing problem in the world. Everyone seems to have an opinion. But I believe that we can find the answers within ourselves.

What is life about anyway? Is it simply a series of lessons and experiences? Do we create our own problems or situations in order to find solutions and answers? Are challenges just a means to discover what works for us—or to cause grief?

Be still and just be. That is my best advice. See if you agree.

ABOUT THE AUTHOR

Patti Angeletti, a published author, has studied angels, reincarnation, past-life regression, crystal therapy, soul contracts, and many other subjects regarding metaphysics. She understands the connectedness we all share and is a student of life on Earth. She shares her gifts of writing, songwriting, prose, and spiritual beliefs in books, music, and workshops. She currently resides in Boise, Idaho, enjoying her children, grandchildren, a dog named Nick, and the world. Her passion is travel. Learn more about her, her books and workshops at: www.starryangel.com

GLOSSARY

There are many topics of a metaphysical or New Age nature mentioned in this book. I have listed them below. I encourage you to discover your own belief system and truths regarding these and other topics by searching outside of yourself in books, libraries, and the Internet. Ask questions of others, attend classes, and participate in lively discussions. Most of all, I encourage you to seek the truth within your own heart and soul and use discernment.

Angels: Spiritual beings believed to act as attendants, agents, or messengers.

Archangels: Angels of high rank.

Astrology: The study of the movements and relative positions of celestial bodies and the interpretation of their influence on human affairs and the natural world.

Connectedness: Joining together with others in a sense of relatedness.

Contracts and agreements: Negotiated arrangements between parties as to certain courses of action.

Crystal therapy: An alternative medicine technique that employs stones and crystals as healing tools

Divine intervention: Active involvement of God and/or angels or other heavenly beings in assisting people.

Dream interpretation: A way of assigning meanings to dreams.

Duality: The quality or condition of being dual.

Free will: The power to act without the constraint of necessity or fate; the ability to act at one's own discretion.

God: Creator of the universe, the Supreme Being. *See also* Higher power.

Guardian angel: An angel specifically assigned to guide and protect an individual.

Higher power: Creator of the universe.

Illusion: Distortion of senses.

Manifesting: Causing something to happen as a result of one's actions.

Near-death experiences: Personal experiences associated with impending death.

Numerology: The branch of knowledge that deals with the occult significance of numbers.

Reincarnation: The rebirth of a soul in a new body.

Soul: The spiritual part of a human being, regarded as immortal.

Soul family: Kindred group of spirits

Spirit: A person's moral or emotional nature or sense of identity.

Spirit world: Habitation of spirits

Totem animals: Animal spirit or essence, used to provide a deeper understanding through lessons or spiritual connection.

Zen: Philosophy, which emphasizes attainment of enlightenment, to favor a direct realization through meditation and dharma practice.

RESOURCES

Doreen Virtue

www.angeltherapy.com

Books:

> *Angels 101: An Introduction to Connecting, Working, and Healing with the Angels*
> *Archangels & Ascended Masters*
> *Messages from Your Angels*

Robert Schwartz

www.yoursoulsplan.com

Books:

> *Courageous Souls*
> *Your Soul's Plan*

Sylvia Browne

www.sylvia.org

Books:

> *Spiritual Connections: How to Find Spirituality Throughout All the Relationships in Your Life*
> *Exploring the Levels of Creation*

Contacting Your Spirit Guide

Brian Weiss, MD
www.brianweiss.com
Books:

Many Souls, Many Masters
Through Time into Healing
Only Love Is Real
Messages from the Masters
Same Soul, Many Bodies

Michael Newton, PhD
www.spiritualregression.org
Books:

Journey of Souls
Destiny of Souls